Invaders From the Dark

Invaders From the Dark

Greye La Spina

MINT EDITIONS

Invaders From the Dark was first published in 1925.

This edition published by Mint Editions 2023.

ISBN 9798888970133 | E-ISBN 9798888970287

Published by Mint Editions®

 **MINT
EDITIONS**

minteditionbooks.com

Publishing Director: Katie Connolly
Design: Ponderosa Pine Design
Production and Project Management: Micaela Clark
Typesetting: Westchester Publishing Services

Contents

Part III

Foreword

S ometime during the latter part of May 1924. I received a communication from a well-known publishing house, a communication sufficiently out of the ordinary to merit, my immediate attention. I had sold these publishers considerable fiction treating of the occult and supernatural; they wrote me to inquire if I were an actual student of the occult, or if I had merely gone into the subject superficially to give more color to my stories. They intimated that there was a special reason back of their inquiry.

I wrote back that I was a serious student of the occult, but that the more I studied it the more I found to learn and the more I realized that I had only scratched the surface of the subject. The publishers wrote back that they had been requested to get in touch with a student of the occult and to ask such a person to communicate immediately with Miss Sophie Delorme, Differdale House, Meadowlawn, Lynbrook. (It is understood, of course, that I am using the fictitious names furnished in the manuscript written by Miss Delorme.)

I was naturally interested and wrote to Miss Delorme at once. The lady informed me that she had a manuscript of about fifty thousand words which she had written to explain an extremely strange matter that, had occurred in her neighborhood. She believed this story to be vitally important and insisted that she dared not entrust the manuscript to any other than a person instructed along occult lines, as she had every reason to believe that efforts would be made to reach and destroy the papers before their message could be transmitted to the world. She asked me to call on her and take over the manuscript personally, and see to it that it was printed.

I ascertained that Miss Delorme was a responsible person, quite able and willing to defray the costs of printing her book, in case it proved to be out of the line of the regular publishing houses. I arranged to visit her home on June 18th, an easy matter, as I found I could get there by subway. On June 18th, therefore, I walked across the fields to the great wall which she had described in her letters, and rang the hell of the bronze gate. From that moment, I began to realize what Miss Delorme meant when she wrote that she feared for the safety of her manuscript.

Even as I stood there waiting, things started to happen in a most bewildering fashion. I heard somebody throw up a window on a side of the house (to my right), and then there came a woman's scream, which sounded to me more angry than fearful. The scream was followed by a heavy, metallic clang upon the pavement just around the corner from where I stood. I left the gate and ran in the direction of the noise.

On the sidewalk lay a black tin box such as is often used to preserve papers of importance. It was dented badly where it had struck the pavement. I picked it up and then I turned my eyes toward the windows above me.

An elderly woman stood at the open window nearest the corner of the house, holding with both hands to the window frame at either side of her. Although she appeared to be alone, I received a strong impression that she was being pulled from behind, for she was struggling as if with all her power, to maintain her position there. As I looked up, the tin box in my hand, she called to me anxiously.

"Who are you?"

I told her.

"Thank God you came in time!" she cried excitedly. "Take the box and get away from here as quickly as you can. Don't let it out of your sight until it has been printed and the books distrubted. You'll understand why, when you've read it. Never mind about me! My work is done!"

As the last words were flung down at me, she disappeared backward into the room, as if pulled there by invisible hands.

I DID NOT DOUBT FOR a moment that I had been talking with Miss Sophie Delorme, and I saw no immediate reason for her lingering in the vicinity. She spoke with a forcefulness that made a strong impression upon me. I felt intuitively that it was of infinity importance for me to leave that spot at once with the tin box and its precious contents. As for Miss Delorme, even if she needed assistance of some kind, I should hardly be able to clamber over that high wall; common sense urged me to call for other help, if it proved necessary.

I hugged the box tightly in my arms and ran away just as fast as I could go, forgetting dignity in my anxiety to carry out the other woman's wishes. Even had I known what was to happen, I doubt if I should have lingered; there are some things in the world of more importance even than a human life, and when one recognizes this fact, one acts upon the knowledge when necessary. I know now that I did well to save the manuscript and to carry out Miss Delorme's desire for its publication. It was well that I stood upon the order of my going, for hardly had I reached the boulevard when a loud and terrible explosion rent the air.

I was flung upon the ground by the force of the concussion, still holding (oh, do not doubt it!) that black box in my arms. When I rose to my feet, dismayed by my premonitions, and turned to look, the Differdale residence with its high surrounding wall no longer marked the spot. A black and smoking mass bulked hugely in its place. Apparently Miss Delorme had not been far wrong when she had warned me that other than human powers would make their attempts to ruin the papers she had entrusted to me; I felt that something had, in a fury of disappointment, brough about her death and ruin of that splendid and strange house, and that this same something would presently be upon my track.

The thought was more than sufficient for me. I rushed down into the subway and caught the next train back to town. Not that this ended the matter. Oh, no! Nor had I imagined that it would. I knew that while the devoted Sophie Delorme's valiant and successful effort to place it in my hands had succeeded, even at the cost of her life, the attempts to destroy it would not cease until they had become futile; that is, until there were enough replicas of the manuscript spread broadcast to make it impossible to suppress the message entirely.

Things became quite too lively from that moment on. I had little time to do more than admire the courage and fidelity of the woman who had undoubtedly perished in the Differdale house, before I was myself involved in one in accident after another. The motorman on the train I caught had a fainting spell and the train ran wild, smashed into the one ahead and broke things up pretty badly. I escaped with the tin box still in my arms, but scratched and cut by flying glass.

I got out at the next station, having walked the subway rails with other passengers, and took a taxi which proceeded to have a blowout and skid into a telegraph post. The driver was thrown out and injured severely, but escaped—with a broken arm. My good arm still held the tin box. When the ambulance came for the driver, I made them take me to my own home. My doctor could not understand why I insisted upon hiding that tin box under the bedcovers, where I could hold onto it. He put my broken on arm into cast, and I had to resign myself to some weeks of inactivity.

I went over the manuscript at the first opportunity, with burning curiosity, I had to have the lock of the box broken open. It was done in presence, of course, but in spite of my repeated warnings, who opened it let his tool slip and drove a hole through some of the sheets, making several words indecipherable. Fortunately, the damage was not great.

Meantime, I negotiated with several publishers for the printing of the manuscript. When I found a publisher, my next difficulty arose. How was I to safeguard it until it was in book form? I explained this to the head of the publishing concern, who provided two watchmen who never for a single instant let the manuscript out of their sight during the day, and at night it was locked into a safe in the presence of two people. Notwithstanding these precautions, things happened. I have never spent such a harrowing, nerve-racking time in my life as I spent last July and August, 1924.

IN SPITE OF THE CARE with which the manuscript was watched, alighted match was dropped upon some of it, and it was saved in the very nick of time. That caused a suggestion that it be typed in duplicate, which was done. During the typing, the young woman typist—whose probity is unquestionable, for she is a personal friend of mine, interested in occult subjects—crumpled up quite a bunch of sheets given her to work from and threw them into the waste basket, by mistake. Fortunately the loss was discovered before too late, and the pages retrieved. The typist cried, she felt so badly about it, and begged that I take charge of the manuscript sheets myself. I dictated it to her, after that, so that the papers did not leave my bands until safely typed.

One copy of these typed pages was shut up in the publisher's safe with the original manuscript; the other was distributed in the print room. A fire broke out in the printing room while the men were out at lunch, and the fire engines came, and the place was drenched, the sheets being almost ruined. Fortunately, we could replace spoiled sheets with clean ones from other copy in the safe.

Then, after the books were printed, the entire printing plant was dynamited, and the books destroyed in the resulting fire. I had taken the proof-sheets home with me, however, and from these I dictated the entire manuscript again to a typist.

I know there are plenty of people who will sneer at the recital of these *accidents*, calling them coincidences, covers a multitude of strange, inexplicable happenings. I know too much those powers who are averse to publishing broadcast the message contained in Miss Delorme's manuscript, to call these occurrences coincidences.

As I write this, I know that Miss Delorme's of warning will go out into the world as she intended, a message for those who can understand. It may be only a piece of fiction for those who are ignorant of what the most casual students of psychic phenomena now consider everyday occurrences. The declaration that there "ain't no ghosts" today is nothing but a display of the speaker's deplorable backwardness in *current news*, alone.

I wish to state, before closing my little foreword, that I have not touched Miss, Belorme's manuscript except to try to separate it into parts, not chapters. It was a single long narrative, as it came to my hands—the writer evidently considered it important to get her message on paper than to divide and subdivide it in the manner of modern letters. I found it awkward to draw any dividing lines in the text, myself.

There is little doubt in my mind that that fine and noble woman lost the veil that separates the human entity from the mysterious and too often malevolent entities of the astral plane. Fortunately for the world—at least for that portion of the world that can understand—she had secured with careful foresight the printing and distribution of her weird and terrible experience, even to the final detail of a large check made out to me and enclosed with the manuscript in the tin box. That she was safeguarded until her work was finished and passed on to me, is proof that other and higher powers of good watched over her while her presence on this plane was necessary.

It is my earnest hope that her sacrifice and devotion will not have been in vain.

Greye La Spina

PART I

I

There is no real reason for the inside history of that summer to and there are strong reasons why it should be made public. I understand fully that many will pronounce the whole affair one of sheer fabrication on my part but on the other hand there are those in are in the world, who will know that my story is not only possible but probable. It is for these last I write, that the knowledge of those strange happenings may put them on their guard; that they may realize the full extent of the danger in this terrible invasion of our dear country by the potent influences of evil that have for centuries flourished in the wild spots of Europe and Asia.

The world ought to know that these forces of the dark are organizing for the advancement of their own individual and collective purposes, just as the forces of light are cooperating for the advancement of humanity; that invasions from the dark will periodically be made—slyly, subtly, whenever opportunity offers; that embodied and disembodied evil upon the New World, intent on conquest. And most terrible of all, the New World is ignorant of these potent influences upon mind and body, attributing the ancient wisdom of the Old World along these lines to the superstitious tales of ignorant peasants.

I know from my own experience that these entities are not figments of the fevered imagination. I know they have arrayed themselves against those who know them and would give them battle. I myself am in deadly peril of their bitter enmity, and one thought only can uphold and strengthen me: God is more powerful than all the combined forces of evil, and while I have a message to give the world, no harm can come to me. When that message has been delivered, my work shall have been finished, and I shall be ready to go, to take up the good fight on another plane of existence.

If I were to relate the whole story in a few terse lines, I am sure that I would be marked down at once as mentally unbalance and thus my effort to gain the ear of *those who can understand* would have failed. I must not shear the tale, then, of any of the trifling incidents, the petty happenings, that will unfortunately give my tale the earmarks of fiction for the uninstructed, but must equally place it beyond cavil as a recital of facts in the opinion of the initiated. I shall, try, therefore, even at the cost of seeming tedious, to relate even the slightest things that may throw light on an as yet comparatively unknown subject upon the existence of which my claim to sanity, as well as that of my niece Portia and that of Owen Edwardes, depends.

The strange and inexplicable disappearance of two police officers from their station; the unsuccessful attack upon a third; the disappearance of a girl of twelve; these incidents may perhaps be recalled to the memory of citizens of a suburban town where they took place, when they read this explanation of those mysterious happenings. It is of course necessary to disguise to a certain extent the names of the principles in the affair, as well as the name of the town itself; I am not writing to satisfy anyone's morbid curiosity or to make Lynbrook—let me call it that—a place of pilgrimage. My sole incentive is to notify the "initiated" in America of what has actually taken place in this New World, of this invasion by the evil powers of the Old World's waste places. This accomplished, I shall feel more than repaid for the effort which it is for me, a woman unaccustomed to writing more than a friendly note, to pen this story which I have an intuition may prove a long one.

Since the heroic deaths, in the World War, of my niece of the Lieutenant Own Edwardes, I have often debated within myself the advisability of setting down an account of those strange and awful happenings, and at last it was borne in upon that I must carry on Portia's work as far as it was possible for me to do so. I lost no time in getting to work, once persuaded where my duty lay.

It is easy to begin, because my part in it really started with Portia's letter inviting me to make my home with her in Lynbrook.

Portia was the only child of my brother Chester, who was killed with his wife in an automobile accident in a day when automobiles were a rarity and not as perfect in their mechanism as they are nowadays. Portia was fifteen at the time. She was left an orphan with little or no means of support, as Chester, manager of the sales department of the Wilton Front Lace Corset Company, had lived up to his income to the last penny. I was, I suppose, the only living relative the child had here in the East, and when I found by inquiry that her mother's people were far from well-to-do-ranchers in Montana and that Portia had scholarly ambitions, I decided to take her to live with me until such time as she married or managed for herself.

When father died, he left the old home in Reading, Massachusetts, with sufficient income to keep it up. Chester had refused to benefit by father's death; he always said he could take care of himself better than a woman could take care of herself. For this reason alone, I felt morally engaged to do what I could for Chester's girl.

Portia came to live with me, then, and attended the public school of Reading and later on went to high school. By the time she had graduated from high school she had already made up her mind what she wanted to do. She intended to go to Vassar, where her father had made application when she was born, as proud parents do nowadays. The only obstacle was the lack of sufficient money to pay her tuition and other expenses. This did not dismay my niece.

Early in her girlhood I had occasion to admire her courage; her absolute fearlessness, rather. She faced the situation of no funds, and made herself mistress of it. The details I do not fully know, but I learned afterward that she eked out the little I managed to send her, by tutoring, by taking down lectures in shorthand and selling the transcribed copies to fellow students. Portia passed her final examinations with high marks and returned to me for a brief period of repose while looking about for a position of some kind.

Just what she was fitted for, she herself did not know. She had thought of library work, but I believe this was merely because she loved books so dearly, not because the career of a librarian appealed to her. Finally she decided her best opportunity might lie in a secretaryship and was about to leave Reading for New York, when a letter arrived one morning, that had been forwarded to her from college.

It was a wonderful morning in early July 1910, when this momentous letter arrived. The sun was no brighter than, my girl's face when lifted it from the letter to exclaim: "Here is the very thing I would have chosen out of all the world, Aunt Sophie, could I have put my wishes into words."

She tossed the letter across the table to me and turned to stare out of the window into the dappled sun and shade of our pretty yard, which I realized she was really not seeing at all.

I took up the letter and read it hastily from one Howard Differdale, of Lynbrook, N.Y., a frank, straightforward statement of his needs. As nearly as I can remember, it ran somewhat in this tenor:

He was a bachelor, living alone in a great isolated house about five city blocks, however, from a community known as Meadowlawn, and near subway lines that made it but half an hour from the heart of Lynbrook. The management of the house was in the hands of a "faithful

Chinaman, Fu Sing." Mr. Differdale was engaged in occult research and experiment and desired a young woman assistant who was not only interested in his line of work but capable of helping materially, and of making the necessary observations in shorthand on the typewriter.

He gave references as to his financial standing. He mentioned that his mother and sister lived in Meadowlawn and attended a Presbyterian church there. He would be glad to pay all expenses for Portia and a chaperon, if my niece were sufficiently interested to make the trip to Lynbrook for the purpose of deciding personally whether or not she desired to take the position he was offering.

The salary he offered was comparatively small, so much so that I wondered at my niece's enthusiasm. The matter of remuneration, however, was taken up later by Mr. Differdale when Portia went down to see him and augmented to an extent that would have made the position a highly desirable one from the financial standpoint, had it been known beforehand. Mr. Differdale explained to my niece a bit dryly that he had purposely made it very small in his letter, because he did not care for the type of woman who would have been attracted for the sake of the remuneration alone; he wanted someone whose strongest motive was the character of the work. But I am getting ahead of the story.

Portia went down to Lynbrook, She did not take me with her. She told me that considered herself capable of judging both the character of the man and the nature of work. She did not return to Reading, but I received a series of letters telling of her arrival, and of various other matters of interest. Some of these I still have, and shall quote here and there to show her first impressions, especially as some of them have a bearing on later events.

With a check, she wrote:

> Dear Aunt Sophie:
>
> I am enclosing a check for my first month's salary in advance, I am sending it all, because I really cannot foresee any particular needs that may arise to necessitate my having on hand more money than the amount of my fare down, which Mr. Ditferdale refunded, as he offered in his letter.
>
> I suppose you would like to know what kind of man my employer is and what the work is for which I am engaged. I am bound by my honor not to divulge the exact nature of the

work, but I can say that it is something which is for the good of all humanity, and that Mr. Differdale can be best judged by this: every penny he derives from an invention of his for weighing and sorting watch mechanism, he devotes to his researches, the nature of which I cannot tell you. His whole life is bound up in carrying on this work.

He is the most absentminded of individuals, when it comes to his personal wants, although his mind is astonishingly alert when it is fixed upon his work. Fu Sing, the Chinese man-of-all-work, has to call him to his meals or I verily believe he would forget that such a thing as food existed. Fu Sing is a model servant, by the way; one never sees him about the house, but he accomplishes wonders in making everything clean and comfortable.

The floors are hardwood with oriental rugs. No chairs; just piles of cushions, I sleep on cushions every night, and I must admit I find it extremely luxurious and comfortable. This is a part of Mr. Differdale's theory; he believes that the part of our lives spent in repose or recreation should be made as relaxing as possible and that complete change is a relaxation in itself. Oh, we need to gain fresh strength daily for the demanding work in which our nights are passed!

Yes, all our work is done at night. So far, I have been out under the stars every night except when it has rained. We sleep all day. I am entering up on an entirely different life, Aunt Sophie, and it is wonderful—and fascinating— and inspiring! I admire my employer hugely; he is really a splendid man. You this just by being in his vicinity; it is a kind of atmosphere spreading about him.

A LATER LETTER READ:

The first week I was here I did nothing but read his books or listen to his explanation of some of the experiments in which I am to assist him later on. I am all impatience, but I cannot help him materially until I have learned many, many things. I am studying now, every minute that I am not sleeping or taking the out-of-door recreation upon which he insists and which is great sport, for it consists in exercising Boris and Andrei (huge white Russian wolfhounds), in the fields that completely surround the high walls of the building where we live in what amounts to isolation.

About five blocks away through the fields lies a little community called Meadowlawn. There are seven or eight solidly built up blocks of brick and stucco houses, bounded on the side nearest us by a wide highway called Queens Boulevard. There are little stores along the boulevard, and the built up streets run at right angles to this wider highway, which is much traveled by trucks and automobiles.

Mr. Differdale took me to call on his mother and his married sister, the afternoon of the day that I arrived, and left me to lunch with them, as he wanted me to get in touch with everybody and everything in his neighborhood, so that I could satisfy myself about his standing. He did not need to do this Auntie; I made up my mind to remain the moment I first laid eyes on him, and he told me afterward that he knew immediately that I was the woman who could help him in his work, when he read my graduation thesis. He had managed to get a hold of several essays by girls in my class, through the dean's influence, and said that he had selected Vassar girl because he believes that Vassar sends out adventurous spirits from her halls!

Mrs. Differdale and Mrs. Arnold do not at all resemble Mr. Differdale, who is invested with a kind of nobility of bearing, a dignity—well, it is something spiritual that you feel about him and that his mother and sister do not possess in the smallest degree. They are both of the earth, earthy; although I'm sure it would hurt their feelings immeasurably to think that anyone considered them other than intensely—well, I'll call it religious, as being apart from spiritual.

Mrs. Differdale is tall and thin with snappy black eyes and frizzed gray hair that she conceals under a soiled boudoir cap mornings when it's in crimpers. She usually removes them before dinner at night, when she dons a silk dress and becomes a lady of leisure. I've found in talking with her that she is intolerant of people who think differently from herself, and very dictatorial from herself, and very dictatorial in stating her opinions as settled facts. She has a curious nature that is really astonishing.

Apropos of her curiosity, she has a trick of catching up a broom and rushing out to sweep the immaculately kept sidewalk on a moment's notice, if any out-of-the-ordinary noise happens to reach her listening ear; and it would be a mighty small noise that didn't, Aunt Sophie, I can assure you. During the two hours I was in her home that first afternoon, she questioned me on about every subject conceivable, but as I was not at all sure of my ground, I managed to evade most of her inquiries, especially those that concerned her son, about whose work she apparently knows quite nothing. She speaks of him with grudging admiration, chiefly because of the money he has made by his invention, it seemed to me.

Her daughter, Aurora Arnold, is as much like the older woman as one pea is like another, except that she is younger. She has thin blond hair and pale blue eyes to which she tries to give an expression of sincerity and sympathy, although she didn't affect me as being what she pretended, and evidently wanted me to believe her. Mr. Arnold works in some kind of machine shop, but she refers to him with a considerable air as a "professional" man. She used to be a kindergarten teacher and—well, you may remember that I always disliked the idea of teaching because of that air of superiority that teachers assume among their pupils until it is second nature. Mrs. Arnold has that air to a degree that, I'm ashamed to admit, I find insufferable.

Like her mother, she is curious about everything and everybody in the neighborhood. I heard more gossip, disguised as friendly criticism, during luncheon time than I've ever heard in all my life before, even in Reading.

I got an impression, vague to be sure, that Mr. Differdale's mother was jealous of my advantage in being his assistant and thus, being admitted to the knowledge of his work. She told me, with rather dry air, that she had never been invited to set foot within the precincts guarded by that ten-foot wall that surrounds the house where her only son lives and works. The thought that I had already been admitted there was only too evidently distasteful to her, and I felt that her disposition to be friendly was motivated by her belief that it would give her latter opportunities to satisfy her curiosity, when more confidential relations should have been established between us.

There are two Arnold children, disagreeable little brats of nine and eleven respectively. Their names are Aliee and Minna. I have rarely had the misfortune to meet such malicious children. I can well believe their mother's complaint that they are always quarreling with other children on that street, but I do not believe it is the others who are at fault, as Mrs. Arnold declares. Their mother says she cannot make them obey her because they are so high-spirited. If this is the actual reason, then deliver me from high-spirited children for the rest of my life! The neighbors appear to share my dislike, for the two children seem extremely unpopular.

Mrs. Differdale asked if her son had provided a chaperon for me and seemed very much put out at what she called his lack of consideration, assuring me that I would undoubtedly find myself very much talked about unless I insisted upon the presence in my employer's house of an older woman whose presence would protect me. I inquired innocently enough if her son had such a bad reputation, and she was quite wild at the insinuation, but kept returning to her observation that people in Meadowlawn were very gossipy.

IN A PREVIOUS LETTER PORTIA described the great square building of two stories that contained the immense laboratory and a roomy library where thousands of ancient and modern volumes were shelved. A dining room furnished in modern fashion, an up-to-date kitchen, and the sleeping quarters of Mr. Differdale, Portia, and Fu Sing, took up the rest of the building. Laboratory, dining room and Fu's kitchen and bedroom were on the ground floor, the library and other sleeping quarters and private bathrooms on the second floor.

Most of Portia's work when she first went there was the indexing for easier reference of thousands of books in the library. The letter from which I quoted at length about Mr. Differdale's family was written about a month after Portia left Reading. From that time on her work must have absorbed her to the exclusion of everything else, for letters became more and more infrequent. The only things I could gleam from theses brief messages were that her employer was a great and noble benefactor of humanity; that she had hurt her knee when racing with the wolfhounds one evening and a Mr. Owen Edwardes (who had a real estate office on the boulevard) had escorted her home, and that the dogs had, "behaved like angels although he was a complete stranger to them"; that Mr. Owen Edwardes had motored her one evening to Pleasure Beach, an amusement resort near Lynbrook—that Owen Edwardes had a really exceptional mind—that Owen had been telling her how he was carrying out his dead father's ideals to build real homes for middle-class families at nominal cost.

I may be an old maid (Portia has since told me that I couldn't be an old maid if I tried, despite my unmarried state, and that the two Differdale woman were typical old maids in spite of being married), but I can scent a romance while it's still a-budding. There was more mention of "Owen" in Portia's letters than any other one thing. It can be imagined, then, that it was like a bolt from the blue to have her write me a quiet, dignified letter without much detail, stating that owing to the neighborhood gossip (which had been strengthened by old Mrs. Differdale in her bitter jealousy of my niece's position of vantage) Howard Differdale and she had been quietly married, so that, as she expressed it, they could carry on their work without interruption or disturbance in the future.

From this time on, Portia's letters became yet rarer. In them, too, there was no mention of Owen Edwardes, although I inquired directly about him twice. I tried to believe that Portia had misled me purposely in writing so much about the young man, in order to cover her infatuation with her employer, but I couldn't seem to reconcile this guile with her letters.

After her marriage, her communications took on a certain dignity and aloofness. It was as if Portia had "put aside childish things." She had suddenly grown up, had come to maturity of mind and spirit. Nevertheless, I could not disabuse my mind of the idea that there had been a close congeniality of mind and spirit between herself and the young man of whom she had written so much before her marriage.

Portia's marriage took place in January 1910, six months after she went to Lynbrook. Her husband's death came very suddenly in December of the same year. She wrote to me no details; merely said that he had been struck down most cruelly in the midst of his work, a victim to the evils from which he had been laboring to save humanity. She added that his death made her prouder of him, if anything, although it was of course a deep loss to her personally as well as to the world, which did not know what it had lost. She intended to carrying on his work, I gathered.

I could not help being troubled at the thought of her in that lonesome spot, with no one but a Chinaman (to whom she referred to as "my faithful Fu") to look after her comfort, and very glad I was when she wrote me in March, proposing that I sell or lease my house and make my home with her.

Perhaps I was getting a bit tired of living alone in a country town. Perhaps I was just plain homesick for the girl whom I had helped bring up. I leased my house and hurried all preparations so that I should be free to go down to Lynbrook at the earliest possible moment.

I must confess that I was also actuated by a burning curiosity as to the nature of the work which my niece admitted had been the death of her husband, and which she continued to carry on, courageously, declaring that it was for the benefit of humanity.

II

My niece met me at the Center Station in Lynbrook, and we took the subway out to the Meadowlawn District.

Portia had changed very much, though very subtly, since she left me a year and a half before. Her blue eyes were dazzlingly clear and looked at one uncompromisingly—there was a mystery in their depths, though. Her straight chestnut hair with its reddish shadows, which she usually wore in a coronet braid, was partially concealed by her black hat, a bit of millinery that cast a dark shade upon her warm brown skin and her glowing cheeks.

She did not look in the least like a sorrowing window. Her manner, her glance, was that of a human being which knows itself so well that it cares little or nothing for the opinions of others. Her figure had grown fuller without being buxom, Portia being the type of woman called magnificent. She had not lost the odd charm of her mouth, which, when slightly parted, showed two upper front teeth a bit; this touch of lightness distracted from her otherwise serious expression, which was the first thing I noted about her.

As we emerged from the subway station upon the street, we were encountered by an elderly woman who inclined her head very slightly in recognition, but with a certain air. Portia touched my arm and stopped me.

"Aunt Sophie, I want to have you meet Mr. Differdale's mother, of whom I've already written you," she said very sweetly.

Mrs. Differdale jerked her head high. She made me think of a superannuated warhorse that hears the military band passing. She almost snorted, in fact, as she acknowledged the introduction. I had an idea that she was embarrassed about something, and Portia told me later that curiosity had made the other woman wait near the subway entrance so that she would be the first to meet me.

"I hope you will be able to persuade your niece to shut up that big, lonely house and live like a civilized human being," she said to me quite sharply. "It's her duty to come out of her seclusion and interest herself in worthwhile work for this community and the world."

Portia did not appear at all disturbed by this little stab, but as we went on her way she remarked, just a bit sadly: "Poor soul, she has never gotten over it that Mr. Differdale left everything to me, except an annuity sufficient for her modest needs. She considers me an interloper, especially as I've obliged to refuse to admit her to the laboratory since my husband's death. She made several visits of condolence within a week."

We walked up about three blocks along Queen Boulevard. Portia pointed out the great ten-foot wall in the middle of the fields. I couldn't have missed it; it was a landmark and a mysterious one at that.

We had just returned up Gilman Street, which runs from the boulevard to the Differdale place, when an automobile came up behind us. The driver stopped it and called Portia's name.

I knew before I was told that this young man with the merry twinkle in his dark gray eyes, the whimsical smile hovering about his generous mouth, and the light brown hair showing under his cap, was Owen Edwardes. I could not refrain from stealing a glance at my niece, but although I imagined I saw a deeper rose creeping up in her blooming cheeks, she maintained a quiet dignity and composure that told me quite nothing.

"Do let me take you home," implored the newcomer, leaning back to open the door for us.

"Aunt Sophie, this is Owen Edwardes," Portia said. "My aunt is going to make her home with me, Owen."

"Aunt Sophie, I'm overjoyed to meet you and to learn that you are going to keep Portia company. I think she needs just you."

Portia smiled slowly. There was a certain gentle enjoyment of this masculine directness in her expression.

"I'm quite contended just now, with my work, Owen," she rebuked. "It is everything to me, you know."

At that, his tone changed.

"You're right, I know," he said with what I interpreted as a touch of bitterness. "You are the most self-sufficient woman I ever knew, Portia. All you have to do is shut yourself away from the rest of humanity in your gray prison, and you're quite happy. No intruding friends for you, eh?"

Then turning to me: "I know it's only a matter of three blocks across the fields, from here, but it's hard walking on the frozen ground. If *you* get in, Portia will have to," he insinuated with an appealing and boyish smile.

I liked him at once, so I go into the automobile, and of course Portia had to follow me. As Owen Edwardes backed the car around, my niece touched my arm and motioned with her head to a woman who, accompanied by two little girls rather strikingly dressed in bright red like twins, walking towards us about a block away.

"That's Mr. Differdale's sister and her children," murmured my niece. "Thanks to you, Aunt Sophie, I'm now giving Aurora Arnold something to gossip about."

I promptly said, "Fiddlesticks!"

Really, I didn't care. I had taken a strong liking to young Owen Edwardes at first sight, and if he showed himself interested in Portia, I didn't intend to put obstacles in the way of his courtship of a charming young widow, in spite of what the neighbors might say.

Mr. Edwardes asked Portia if there were anything he could do for her, before he went. He offered to go to the Center Station for my trunk and bad, instead of leaving them to come over by express. Of course, I refused his offer, but I told myself that unless he were interested in Portia he wouldn't have offered to go so much out of the way for me.

PORTIA PRESSED A BELL BUTTON inserted in the deep wall beside the heavy bronze door that presently swung open before her key, the bell being to notify Fu Sing that she had retuned, so that he could regulate the hour for serving dinner accordingly. For a moment I had a feeling of panic when I heard that great door clang shut behind me. I remembered all at once that in this enclosure some mysterious work was carried on: that somewhere here, inside those insurmountable walls. Howard Differdale had dropped dead under Portia's very eyes, almost at her side. I couldn't help shuddering.

The next moment Portia had thrown her arms around my neck and her warm kiss fell upon my neck.

"Welcome home, dearest Aunt Sophie!" she was crying.

Her words, her voice, her kiss, swept unpleasant associations out of my mind, and I followed her cheerfully enough across the wide courtyard to the massive granite building that was to be my home in future. The house door was opened to us by the bowing, smiling Fu Sing, sucking in his breath in excruciatingly polite manner as he retreated before us.

Portia took me at once to my room on the second floor. It was wonderfully attractive, except that it had no bed, only a pile of silken cushions. She asked me if I wanted to try the cushions, or if she should telephone in Lynbrook for a regulation bed. It happens that I really do like to try new things, so I vetoed her suggestion at once;

I thought I might enjoy playing that I was in some kind of Eastern palace.

At dinner, which was served in a handsome, entirely modern dining room that opened off the kitchen through a butler's pantry. Portia tried to give me a brief resumé of the events of the year covered by her married life. I shall put it into a few words just at this point in my narrative.

Quite without the slightest attempt at concealment, she told me that she and Owen Edwardes had come close to having an understanding, but that what she had learned of her employer's work had decided her that so long as Howard Differdale needed her, it would be her joy as well as her duty to work beside him. She had given Owen to understand this, delicately, as a woman can.

And then Mrs. Differdale had written her son a venomous note, quite as wicked as only so-called good, religious people could have made it. Mr. Differdale had quietly put the matter before my niece. As between his work and any personal inclinations, his work stood first, he told her. He needed her presence in his experiments; he felt the necessity of her aid in his work. But he would not take advantage of her interest, her good heart, at the expense of her reputation. When she indignantly declared that she would remain because she believe his work the most important thing that had come into her life, he asked her to permit him to give her his name.

"I married him, Auntie, but our marriage was nothing more than a wall of protection that we put up between our work and the malicious tongues of people in Meadowlawn. Mr. Differdale never made the slightest claim upon me as a husband. You see, Auntie, in order to be of assistance to him, I had to remain a maid; only a virgin can help in such experiments as he was carrying on."

As can well be imagined, I was interested by this simple statement of a rather astonishing situation. I inquired, tentatively, about the nature of this work to which Portia now referred as "ours" instead of "his." She tried to explain it, I could see, in some general fashion, but I found myself in such a daze after her explanation that I gave up trying to understand it, quite it despair.

I did glean, however, that Mr. Differdale was what she called "an initiate"; that he had gone deeply into occultism and the practice of magic; that he had actually performed incantation to call spirits into materialization, out in that great courtyard where I had seen mystical hieroglyphics cut into the stone. I learned, too, that he had come to his death because in over-excitement he had forgotten for a single moment that he must never overstep the limits of a circle within which he performed his spells. One night, my niece told me with perfect gravity, he had gone outside that circle, and Portia, standing beside him, had seen the results of the terrible blows which he must have received from invisible hands (the newspapers had it that he had fallen from a window during a sudden attack of dizziness).

The whole matter was so weird, so unbelievable, that my tired brain almost refused to accept it; I found myself wondering if my nieces' brain had not been turned. But I was astonished at my own mental attitude when I discovered that in my new and strange surroundings I was deliberately trying to digest Portia's tale as gospel truth, taking it at her valuation. When I went with her after dinner into the great library and handled some of the curious old books, many in Latin and other foreign languages, and noted their queer titles, I began to swallow her story in great gulps, explaining away the difficult parts as things that I might not understand at the moment but should shortly be in a position to clear up for my logical, disbelieving mind.

The following morning I suggested to Portia that she let me do the marketing, which she or Fu Sing had previously done by telephone. I wanted to occupy my time, and this appeared to me the most sensible thing for a woman of my habits; it would give me a little walk each morning, and it is human nature for a tradesman to give you better service when you appear in person than when you are nothing but a voice heard daily over the telephone. Portia did not care; she told me to do exactly as I chose, if it made me happy and contended. I got the name of her tradespeople and about nine o'clock went out with my list of needed articles.

Directly opposite where Gilman Street adjoins the boulevard I saw a little building about twelve feet square, with gold lettering on the door: Owen Edwardes, Successor to A.J. Edwardes, Real Estate.

It have me quite a comfortable feeling to know that the young man's office was so close at hand. A silly thought, perhaps, being quite illogical, but I felt it just the same. An automobile was standing outside and as I crossed the boulevard Owen himself came out and locked his office door. Then he looked up and took off his hat to me with a smile that warmed my heart, it was so frank and pleased-looking.

"Well, if here isn't Aunt Sophie!" said he gayly. "What is she wandering about for, so early in the morning?"

"I am going to do the marketing Mr. Edwardes," said I, trying hard to be severe with him, for he really hadn't the slightest right to call me Aunt Sophie, although I believe Portia had not introduced me as Miss Delorme.

"Please don't frown on me so! I can't bear to start the day with a scowl," he implored whimsically. "And you pity's sake don't call me Mr. Edwardes. I can only be Owen to Aunt Sophie."

How could anybody maintain dignity with such a rogue? I laughed outright, whereat he joined me with goodwill.

"Now, I call that fine, Aunt Sophie. We're good friends now, aren't we? Now that we've laughed together? Let me take you down to the butcher's or the baker's or wherever you're headed, won't you? I'm going that way myself—have to call on a Russian princess who's buying a house from me."

I hesitated. There would in all likelihood be further inferences drawn from my seeming familiarity with this pleasing young man. But, after all, the harm must have been done the evening before, for Portia had quite indifferently observed that most of the neighborhood gossip had its fountainhead at the Differdale-Arnold home on Elm Street. I got into the automobile, assisted by the affable Owen, who insisted upon covering me up as carefully as if we were starting for a long drive.

He let me out at the butcher's, about six blocks off. I noticed everybody seemed to know him, hailing him cordially and familiarly as we went along. Even the policeman opened the door of his little station opposite the butcher store, and shouted a facetious greeting. I thought he said something about going to see the princess, and not to be too proud of his swell friends; to which Owen called back as he started away, that he'd introduce O'Brien to the princess as soon as she settled in the neighborhood.

Poor O'Brien, looking so straight and robust in his blue uniform! How little did he dream then under what circumstances he was to meet the Russian princess!

That morning I made the acquaintance of Mike Amadio, the Italian fruitier and green-grocer, and of Gus Stieger, the butcher. I left my orders, stating that I would call two or three times a week at least for the purposes.

WHEN I WAS RETURNING, I met and recognized by their red dresses the two little Arnold girls, both of whom stuck their small noses pertly into the air at the sight of a stranger, and went by me with the most impudent expressions on their faces. Had they been mine, I would have spanked them soundly for their insolence, but from what Portia had written me, I felt sure their mother would commend them for having shown their "high spirits." I must add that I was so astonished at the behavior of the two children who at ten and twelve years should have known better, that I actually turned around as they passed me, distrusting my own eyes, and Minna stuck out her red tongue at me with considerable gusto.

I have always been rather glad that I did not feel anything but an itching desire to spank Minna, or I might have been conscience-stricken later on. But again, I'm getting ahead of my story. It is hard to get everything into its proper sequence, when one is looking back and can understand things that at the time seemed out of place and inexplicable.

I walked briskly back to the house without any other experiences, rang the bell, and was admitted by Fu Sing, who bowed and scraped his way backward as I entered. He informed me in his heathen dialect that "Missee" was in the "Libelly," which information I was unable to understand until my own inclinations drove me to resort to Mr. Differdale's books, there being really nothing else for me to do except read. There I found my niece lying comfortably among her silken cushions, absorbed in a black-covered volume with queer-looking circles and triangles on the cover.

She glanced up as I came in and closed the book.

"Did you enjoy your marketing expedition? I so dislike running into Mrs. Differdale or Aurora, or those two insufferable children, that I'm coward enough to resort to the telephone," she observed lazily.

I tried to let myself down gracefully onto the cushions and failed dismally.

"I've simply got to make some loose flowing robes like yours, Portia," said I.

"They're ever so much more comfortable than ordinary clothes, Auntie," said my niece dreamily.

Just then I suddenly took note of a detail that had escaped my attention. It had been so becoming, and it seemed so natural to me, that I hadn't noticed it. Portia's negligee or whatever you could call it was not black nor did it have a touch of crape about it; instead, it was some kind of shimmering orchid shade over a metallic and shiny green, not mourning at all.

"Why, Portia!" I exclaimed. "You're not dressing in mourning are you, my dear?"

She looked down at her flowing garments, regarded them quietly for a moment, then raised her eyes to mine.

"I don't believe in putting on black, Auntie, and neither did Mr. Differdale"—(I realized then for the first time, that she had never called him by his first name to me)—"I do put it on to go out around Meadowlawn, for the sake of his mother and sister, who would believe otherwise that I was not showing proper respect to his memory. I do not wish anyone to think that I am not respecting sufficiently the memory of that splendid man—but her—in the privacy of my own home, may I not relax sufficiently to permit myself the relief of this color, instead of wearing depressing black?"

"What do you wear at night, when you exercise Boris and Andrei?" I inquired. Boris and Andrei were the wolfhounds to whom I had been introduced that morning, and who had shown a decided disposition to be friends with me.

"I wear whatever happens to be handy," Portia answered, with a slight curl of her fine lips. "Frequently I wear riding breeches when I go out with the dogs at night, as I am freer to run that way than I would be in skirts. Of course, I try to avoid Meadowlawn people; they'd be scandalized at such a costume," she added, shrugging her shoulders.

"Owen took me down to the butcher's in his automobile," I informed my niece. "He was on his way to call on a Russian princess."

III

Portia sat up suddenly on her cushions, betraying a tense interest in what I was telling her.

"The Princess Tchernova?"

"He only said a Russian Princess Portia. Your butcher pointed out a very interesting house and beautifully landscaped grounds, some distance farther along the boulevard, which he told me the lady was on the point of acquiring."

"I'm sorry," Portia exclaimed, half to herself, as if in answer to some secret thought.

I regarded her with astonishment.

"Why sorry, my dear?"

"Well, really, Aunt Sophie, it would be hard to say just why I'm sorry that the Princess Irma Andreyevna Tchernova has decided to settle permanently in this neighborhood. I—I really don't like the lady."

"You have met her then?"

"At Owen's office a couple of weeks ago. I was passing, and she was just going back to her automobile, so Owen insisted upon introducing her. She was—oh it's quite impossible to put one's intuitions into words. She was—well, decidedly exotic, you know."

"What did she look like, Portia? Pretty?"

I began to have a fain suspicion that Portia's dislike for the Russian might be founded upon an unacknowledged jealousy.

"Pretty!" cried my niece. "She is one of the loveliest, and at the same time most evil, creatures I have ever seen in all my life."

"You haven't lived very long," I reminded her dryly. "You're only going on twenty-five now, you know."

"She has dead-white skin," Portia continued reminiscently. "Her mouth is like a crimson stain across that milky whiteness. Delicately flaring nostrils, like a spirited horse's. Her hair is ash-blond and she wears it drooping over her small ears, which must be low-set or they wouldn't show beneath at all."

"I must confess I can't see what extreme loveliness there is in your Princess What-you-call-her, if she has a chalky complexion and wide nostrils, and—"

Portia turned on me.

"I wish to heave she weren't so exquisitely lovely!" cried she with passion. "It's not right! It's not fair, that such as she. . . oh, Auntie, you would have to see her to understand how fascinating she is!"

"Well, go on, Portia, and tell me more of her loveliness," I begged ironically.

"There's something about her light-hazel eyes that I can't quite understand, unless. . . but then, I don't see how that could be probably," she corrected herself vaguely.

"You are really making yourself very clear, Portia."

"I mean that when she looked down so that her eyes were in shadow, or when the shade of her wide-brimmed fur hat fell across her face, there was a warm light in her eyes that was almost, if not quite, garnet. I didn't—I don't—like that, Aunt Sophie."

"She must be an albino, if she has pink eyes," I snapped.

"But they're not pink. Her eyebrows, too—they're finely penciled and several shades darker than her hair. They curve downward until they meet in a sharp angle over her thin, delicately modeled nose. She shows her teeth too much when she smiles, too," mused my niece.

"Do you mean that she has a 'gummy' smile?" I insinuated.

"Oh, no, not at all. Her teeth just show a little, but they are small—and glittering white—and sharp. She has a trick of moistening her red lips with her pointed little tongue."

"It seems to me that you were very observant, when one considers that you've only met the lady on a single occasion," I observed. "She must be almost as unpleasant as those Arnold children," said I, recalling my encounter with those disagreeable and precocious infants.

"Her hands are slender, fascinating, with polished almond-shaped nails. I wish I could have seen enough of them in repose to have noted the length of the third fingers."

"It sounds to me as if you thought you were on track of something, Portia."

"I believe I am, Auntie! The more I think of it—"

She jumped up from her cushions, managing her flowing draperies with an easy grace that I envied, and went browsing about among the books, taking out first one, then another, and laying them aside. Afterward she brought them across the room, made a little pile beside her cushions, and sank down near by.

She began then to turn their pages so absorbedly that I went up to my own room after a little while and began to unpack my trunk, which had arrived that morning during my absence. It was just as well that I busied myself without depending upon Portia for distraction; she hardly spoke during lunch, after which she returned at once to her books, making notes here and there as she read.

IT WAS LATE IN THE afternoon when she apparently finished whatever she was looking up. I had walked past the library door a couple of times, and peeped in to see if she was through.

She came up to my room, yawning widely.

"After more than a year of sleeping all day, it's hard to overcome the habit," she said, stretching luxuriously as she halted on the threshold.

"Why don't you take a little nap?"

"Because I'm trying to keep regular hours like yours, Aunt Sophie. Still. . . .oh, you can have no idea how much I miss Mr. Differdale! The uplift, the inspiration of his companionship, his work! If I could only have an opportunity to talk to him right now," said she tensely, "how thankful I'd be! He could solve my problem so quickly and easily—and I don't know that I am prepared to undertake his work and carry it on alone, yet."

"For the Lord's sake, keep away from those magic spells you've been telling me about, Portia Delorme!" I cried in considerable alarm.

The very idea of her raising—figuratively, if not actually—the devil, made me sick with apprehension. I thought of her late husband's dreadful fate, and shuddered.

"Oh, don't be afraid Auntie. I'm not going to take any risks if I can help it. But I certainly should like to talk with him," she finished musingly.

At this juncture Fu Sing came trotting up into the hallway to remark that the automobile of the honorable Mr. Edwardes was without, and that the honorable Mr. Edwardes wanted to know if the distinguished ladies wouldn't like a little spin up the boulevard to the bay, as the day was so springlike.

My niece was very much pleased, I could see, but she sent back word that she regretted that her work had piled up so that she couldn't take advantage of Mr. Edwardes' kind offer, but that her aunt would be delighted to accept, I was provoked with her, but then. . . how were other people to know that the marriage between herself and Howard Differdale was nothing but a business partnership? At least, she owed him the respect of not entertaining the attention of another suitor for a few months.

Owen (he would have it that I must call him that) had the diplomacy to make me feel that my presence was what he had particularly desired. He tucked me in warmly and we went rolling along up the boulevard. We didn't talk much, for there was really very little to say, but he had the faculty of making you think that he was all the time considering your comfort. If I had married. I should have liked a husband like Owen. I thought to myself, that if this attitude was sincere, he ought to make mighty agreeable husband for someone, and couldn't help wondering just what Portia was going to do with him, for that he was at her disposal I hadn't the slightest doubt.

AT A POINT WHERE THE boulevard turned into Bayside Avenue, he stopped the car so that I could enjoy the sight of the sun glittering on the waters of the bay. I leaned back, drinking in deep drafts of the balmy air with its promise of spring. A limousine with a fur-swathed chauffeur drew up alongside and Owen took off his hat, smiling that irresistible smile of his. The occupant of the other ear pressed a button, and then leaned across the opening made by the dropped window-glass.

It was a woman, swathed in rich furs so completely that at first sight I could hardly distinguish more than the warm glitter of her eyes. At sight of them. I recalled Portia's description of the Russian princess, for those eyes glowed with a ruddy gleam that certainly made them seem garnets in the deep shadow of the enveloping sables.

"Ah, Ow-een, how charming, this so-spring day!" trilled the woman's voice blithely, with a thrilling undernote of rich meaning that made my backbone stiffen involuntarily. That woman called him "Owen!" And with what an intonation!

"Aunt Sophie," at once exclaimed Owen, with a possessive air as he indicated me to the occupant of the limousine, "permit me to present the Princess Tchernova. My adopted aunt, Miss Sophie Delorme."

The princess pushed out slender, taper-tipped fingers with pretty impulsiveness. She appeared to take it for granted that she must be very much persona grata with anybody whom she chose to honor with her friendship.

"Ah, now I begin to feel myself so with Ow-een's dear Aunt Sophie for a friend!" she exclaimed with what in any other woman would have been called gush, but was only delightfully friendly coming from her. "In my new home, I shall not be lonely, for I have the good friends about me, already, is it not? Yes, Ow-een?"

"Right princess," my escort said heartily.

She thrust that slender white arm yet farther from the protecting furs and laid her outstretched fingers possessively on Owen's sleeve. My eyes followed the motion, as I thought to myself that the princess was either much interested in the young man or as a finished coquette. And then I ascertained an interesting fact, one that I felt would prove highly entertaining for Portia; the third finger of that patrician hand was so much longer than the middle and index fingers that it amounted to an abnormality.

"Ow-een, have I not tell you that you must say the friendly 'Irma' to me, not the cold 'princess.' Ah, bad boy, how fast you forget a woman's words! It is doleful, is it not, *chére* Aunt Sophie?"

I jerked my eyes away from that strange hand with an effort, and met her keen glance. I knew immediately that she had seen and understood my absorption. She withdrew the hand with a slow, caressing movement, half smiling at me meantime with an odd significance that made me hot all over for some reason. First of all, I was displeased at her calling me aunt—even for a woman of her undeniable charm and aristocracy, it was an unwarrantable liberty. And then her expression when she smiled! I could not explain why, but it was as if she had suddenly taken me into her confidence in some secret matter in which she expected my tacit acquiescence and approval.

I could not reply to her implied expectancy of an affirmative answer: my blood must have flush my face noticeably, for she all at once turned her gaze from me with a glitter of those hazel eyes, which now seemed almost green as she leaned away from her sables and out into the sunlight. Her lips parted, ever so little, disclosing sharp white teeth, beautifully regular. I suppose most people would have said that her smile was charming, but I know that when she smiled at me I felt only a dreadful sinking feeling, a kind of growing terror, blind terror at I knew not what. I leaned back in the automobile with a sickness in my heart that suddenly took all the beauty out of the delightful day.

"I could not resist to look at the new home, Ow-een," purred the princess, drawing her furs about her sinuous body with the hand that she now kept hidden beneath those luxurious folds. "I have already send the furnitures, so that I may live here, with my so-dear friends close by—soon—soon."

How those words lingered on her red, red lips! An involuntary shudder gripped me and made me tremble. I felt premonitions of evil;

shook them off angrily: felt them return stronger than before at the princess' little side glance at me, a glance half amused, wholly tolerant, as of one who knew her innate powers but disdained to use them upon so entirely insignificant an individual. She moistened her full crimson lips with a pointed little tongue and addressed herself again to Owen.

"When I make the house-warm, my Ow-een, you will be my guest? And the beautiful Mrs. Differdale? And of course, the *chére* Aunt Sophie."

Delicate raillery sounded in her well-modulated voice. She sank back languidly into the brocaded interior nodded her head like a queen dismissing her court, and was whirled away.

OWEN DREW A DEEP BREATH and turned to me, eyes sparkling.

"Some princess, eh, Aunt Sophie? The Princess Irma Andreyevna Techernova. Isn't she a wonder? Won't it wake things up to have her in the neighborhood? She and Portia ought to be great friends, don't you think? Two such brilliant women," he went on fatuously.

I was furious. I suppose I showed it in my voice and manner. I remarked "coldly that the princess had not impressed me especially as being anything but a finished coquette. Of course I should not have said that; men are proverbially obtuse where pretty women are concerned, and Owen was no exception to the rule.

"Why, Aunt Sophie!" he gasped, evidently astonished at my bitter attack upon the Princess Tchernova.

"Don't 'Aunt Sophie' me, young man!" I responded, somewhat tartly. "I have no intention of being an aunt to everybody in this vicinity."

I regretted my abruptness the moment I had spoken, for Owen turned genuinely hurt eyes to me.

"Do you really mind me calling you 'Aunt'?" he asked.

"I don't mind you," I qualified, "But I don't see why that—that Russian—should call me 'Aunt.'"

He smiled.

"I'm glad you don't mind *me* Aunt Sophie, for I want you to know that I'm hoping, some day, really to be your nephew."

His dark gray eyes sparkled and his lips compressed determinedly as he looked honestly into my eyes.

I couldn't help it. I leaned forward and patted the arm that lay across the seat in front of me. Owen did an odd thing for an American; he caught up my hand and touched his lips to it very gently. Then he started up the car and without any further conversation we turned back, for a slightly chilly wind was springing up.

When he helped me out, he took both my hands in his and stood for a moment without speaking, his eyes on mine. Then, "Be my friend with Portia, Aunt Sophie," he said in a low voice, dropped my hands and went away without looking back.

PORTIA WAS SLEEPING WHEN I returned, and did not waken until long after dinner, which I had to eat alone, as Fu Sing managed to explain my niece had given orders not to be disturbed. She came into the library about ten o'clock that night, just when I was telling myself that I ought to go to bed. She was looking especially beautiful, it appeared to me; a wholesome beauty that did my heart good, not that exotic, evil loveliness possessed by the Russian.

"Well, Aunt Sophie, did you and Owen have a heart-to-heart talk this afternoon, and get things nicely settled?"

Her question brought my eyes smartly to her mischievous face.

"Portia Delorme!"—(I never could remember her married name to say it at proper time)—"Just what do you mean to insinuate?"

"Oh, nothing, Auntie."

But she laughed as she flung herself across a pile cushions opposite.

"If you really want to know," I said with dignity, "that young man is deeply interested in you."

Portia fumbled with tassels that adorned her negligee, eyes downcast.

"I'm not so sure of that, Auntie. He's—he's been rather taken up by the Princess Tchernova since she's been haunting his office of late."

"She's nothing but a client," I reminded her.

And then there flashed into my mind a picture of Princess Irma's slender white hand, with that strange finger.

"Portia, she has the oddest hand I've ever seen. Her third finger is so long that—"

"Auntie Sophie, are you sure?"

My niece had suddenly grown extraordinarily grave. She sat up among the cushions stiffly, her lips parted tensely.

I described the Russian's hand minutely. I tried, rather stumblingly, to impart the impression (so fleeting, so vague, but so definitely unpleasant) that her intimate smile had made upon me, and finished by saying with considerable acidity that she was the most perfect specimen of finished flirt I had ever met.

Portia, who had listened without interrupting me while I described the princess' hand, suddenly flashed into vivid life at my last words.

"Ah! And Owen? I mean, how does it appear to him? Does he—is he letting that—creature beguile him?"

It was so natural, that touch of woman's jealousy, that I felt like smiling, but controlled my features by an effort.

"Owen Edwardes is a young man whom it would be hard to persuade into believing evil of any woman," I told Portia thoughtfully.

"In other words, Own is letting that woman fool him with her studied wiles? Oh, and I can do nothing, quite nothing! I am tied down, quite helplessly, by the respect I owe to Mr. Differdale's memory!"

"Why, Portia, is it as bad as all that?" I said stupidly, as I saw her fling out clenched hands with a gesture of desperation.

She laughed shortly, recovering her poise as abruptly as she had just lost it.

"Yes, Aunt Sophie, it's as bad as that," she echoed. "I love him. I loved him from the time we first met. But—"

"You loved him, and you let your wretched work come between you?" I exclaimed reproachfully. I may be an old maid, but I could not appreciate my niece's strange attitude.

Portia turned her grave face upon me.

"You see, Aunt Sophie, you don't entirely understand the nature of the work Mr. Differdale was doing. If you did, I'm sure you would have been the first to advise me to sacrifice everything else in the world for just that."

Her voice rang with earnestness, but I shook my head slowly, I had to admit that I couldn't conceive of any work that would be so important as to be allowed to stand between two eminently suitable young people who cared for each other as I felt she and Owen cared.

"You see, you don't understand," Portia repeated insistently, "and then, later on, I married—and it was too late."

"And now, you're so particular to pay public respect to a man who wasn't your husband, only your business partner, that you cannot even give Owen the satisfaction of some kind of an understanding, so that he won't be on pins and needles during the months of your—widowhood?"

I suppose I did say that in a very nasty manner. I couldn't help it. I was exasperated with Portia. But she did not seem angry at my words or my manner. Instead, she began fussing again with a tassel.

"I suppose I might do something like that," she admitted.

I was jubilant.

"Of course, you know I cannot be seen with him in public for sometime to come, and it wouldn't be wise to have him calling here for a while yet," she went on, musingly.

"You're thinking of that old Differdale female, aren't you? And your husband's sister? And the rest of the Meadowlawn gossips? Shame on you, Portia Delorme!"

She laughed right out then.

"You're an incorrigible matchmaker aren't you Auntie? Well," she added lightly, "we'll see what can be done in the matter."

"I'm going to bed," I said rather shortly, rather disgusted at the indifferent way in which she seemed to take things. "You can stay here and laugh over that boys' love, if you wish."

"Aunt Sophie, I've got other things to do that sneer at the honest love of a man whom I—of whom I think as highly as I do of Owen. I've been sleeping this afternoon because I've work to do tonight, and it's time now that I began it. Fu Sing is fixing me something to eat, and then—"

"You're going to do that—that?"

"Auntie, don't you realize that Mr. Differdale was taken away just at the zenith of his powers and knowledge, with his work unfinished? I've got to carry it on; it's up to me. Especially since the Princess Andreyevna Tehernova is going to settle in this neighborhood."

So stern, so uncompromising was her intonation, that I got right up off my cushions, kissed her a bit timidly, and scooted up to my room. Yes, scooted is the right word; I felt that my room was going to be a haven of refuge for me that night, as far as possible from open courtyard where Portia might later be carrying on her strange performances.

I COULDN'T HELP THINKING, AS I put my hair into crimpers (Portia likes it better waved und it's quite the same to me) that my niece was going a little too far in her jealousy of the beautiful foreigner. A coquette the princess might be, but now that I tried to look at the matter without prejudice, if she were infatuated with Owen, it was no one's business but her own if she attempted to win his affection. Of course, as Portia's friend I didn't want the princess to succeed, but if Owen were to prefer Irma to Portia, and Portia didn't feel like lifting a finger to hold him, it was Portia's loss and Irma's gain.

I went to bed, wondering only what my niece would be doing throughout the long night hours. I had my suspicions. As for me, I slept splendidly, in spite of a heavy electrical storm that must have come up in the middle of the night, for when I went to the market the following morning, there were traces of the destruction wrought, such as many trees with broken boughs. One telegraph pole and all the wires attached to it lay across the side street running parallel with Gilman street.

Gus Stieger, Portia's estimable if expensive butcher, beamed happily at me as I waited for him to finish a big order he was just preparing.

"Let it wait, let it wait, ma'am. I'm just cutting off the tough pieces"—he winked atrociously—"for the Russian lady's wolves. That's sure going to be fine business."

"The Russian lady's wolves?" I echoed somewhat at a loss, until the truth flashed across me and I interpreted his facetiousness aright. "Oh, you mean the Princess Tehernova, don't you?"

"Uh-huh, she's movin'—today into that there big house and she's brought a cage with five big gray wolves, for pets."

A huge laughed widened his good-natured mouth.

"Ain't that a good one, though?" he added. "Wolves for pets!"

I gave him my order and went over to the grocer's. Mike Amadio appeared somewhat disgruntled, and upon inquiry I found that he was as disgusted and disappointed in the newcomer as Gus had been delighted.

"'No bread! No sugar! No butter! No eggs!'" mourned Mike with expressive hands a-spread in gesticulation. "No salads! No vegetables! What does the lady eat, I want to know!" disgustedly. "Just meat—and meat—and meat! Red, bloody meat! Like a savage, that proud lady eats nothing but meat. Gus has told me what quantities he sends to where she has been boarding. Pounds and pounds of bloody meat everyday!"

"Perhaps she has some savage Russian pets, Mike," I suggested.

Evidently, Mike had not thought this. He nodded with sullen acquiescence, but I could see that he was much disgruntled. It was apparent that the tradesmen in Meadowlawn had been making their plans with regard to the newcomer and were being sadly disappointed. It seemed that the Princess Tehernova was not a tremendously large consumer of fancy groceries, greens, or dairy products.

"Two servants," grumbled Mike, selecting romaine for my order. "A big man who goes around in a fur coat like a walking bear. And an old woman with bare feet, *signorina*. Bare feet!"

IV

I told Portia when I got home (she came out at my entrance, heavy-eyed from loss of sleep) about Mike's complaints, merely as indicative of the attitude of the tradespeople, and as a matter of humourous interest. To my surprise, she appeared to take it seriously, questioning me about the item of the meat and the lack of other staples such as salt and sugar with a pointed interest that roused my curiosity.

Fu Sing brought in a tray with a light salad and a pot of tea, and Portia ordered it taken into the library, where she let herself down wearily upon a pile of cushions, her odd breakfast on a tabouret in front of her.

"I wish I were a man," she remarked, poking aimlessly at the salad. "I mean, of course, a man like Mr. Differdale. It is very hard for a woman, especially for me, feeling as I do about Owen, to undertake what I fear must be undertaken, now that the Princess Irma has actually come to stay in Meadowland. I doubt my own powers. I fear my own impulses. I would give anything—anything—for a talk with *him*."

I knew whom she meant by that "him"; she was referring to the man who had given her his name that he might carry on his work uninterruptedly, a thing that I could not help regarding as a stupendous piece of egotism, no matter what my niece thought about it.

"You see," went on Portia, her smooth brow crinkling a bit as she looked up to meet my eyes with frank sincerity, "people will think I'm jealous, and Aunt Sophie, you must believe me with all your heart when I tell you I'm not jealous. That is, not as people interpret jealousy. No, if Owen can be happier with another woman, I would be the first to wish him joy. I love him enough for that. But—oh, it must not be Irma Andreyevna Tchernova! No, no!"

The sudden passion in her voice, the actual horror that now writhed across her tortured face, startled me.

"Why, Portia, my dear! Whatever put the princess into your mind as a rival?" I said stupidly.

She stared at me for a minute without speaking.

"It's my opinion that the princess is just an idle woman who is looking for a flirtation to pass away the time. She's the type of woman who wants a good-looking man always hanging about her, Portia. I don't think she's really interested in Owen."

"Oh, these unutterably narrow-minded Meadowlawn people!" cried my niece, suddenly veering about in another direction. "If only they were not so contemptibly small-minded! If they would only not believe me disrespectful to Mr. Differdale's memory, I should be free to let Owen put his ring on my finger. Then—perhaps—that woman—"

"My dear Portia, why don't you tell Owen that you are willing to be engaged to him, privately, until such time as the properties would consider it good form to announce the engagement publicly?"

"Aunt Sophie! If I am going to be engaged to Owen, I'm not going to hide it from the world as if I were ashamed of our love. I won't carry on a clandestine love affair. No, no! There ought to be someother way!"

She poured herself another cup of tea.

"You and I are going to take a walk with Boris and Andrei tonight," she said, all at once, as if she had made up her mind to something. "We'll go up across the subway bridge back of the house, and down by the Old Burnham place which the princess has taken. Wolves for pets—it's strange."

Her inferences left me deeply stirred. It was if she had made a conclusion that she could not put into words. She did not mention the matter again, changing the subject to one of summer clothes, which she thought we'd better be thinking about soon, for spiring would be shortly upon us.

After breakfast, Portia went to her room leaving me to my own devices. I began to realize that I was going to be very much alone, and that it might be wise on my part to associate myself with some church in the vicinity, in order to form a little circle of acquaintances. I thought it would only be decent, under the circumstances, for me to make a little call on Mrs. Differdale and her daughter, and make the inquiry of them; they would undoubtedly be full advised as to what their denominations were. About half past three o'clock, then, I went out, leaving word with Fu Sing (Portia had apparently gone to sleep again to make up for her night's wakefulness) that I would return about five.

WHEN I WALKED UP ELM Street, Mrs. Differdale stood on the porch steps, wrapped in a shawl. In the cellar-area, holding a pair of her husband's old trousers about her head, the suspenders dangling strangely about her ears, stood Aurora Arnold, absorbedly listening to Gus Stieger. When Mrs. Arnold caught sight of me, she rightly inferred that I was about to call, and disappeared into the cellar with her interesting and original headdress hastily pulled down out of sight. Her mother did not see me until I was almost at the foot of the steps. I could hear Gus plainly.

"Meat. Great hunks of bloody meat, she orders for the wolves," he was saying with unction. "Big gray fellows they are, that snarl and bare their yellow teeth at you. I'll say I'd hate to be near if one of 'em got out. How do, Miss Delorme?"

He touched his hat hastily, crossed to the curb, mounted his bicycle and rode away.

"Come right in, dear Miss Delmore," Mrs. Differdale hastened to say cordially. "You'll excuse my hair being in curlers, and my boudoir cape, I know. There's a church social tonight, and you know, it's one's duty to look one's best in the house of the Lord."

As she ushered me in at the front door, her daughter rushed up the front stairs precipitately. She did not meet my eyes and I pretended not to have seen her. She was certainly a sight, curlers sticking out all over her head, and those trousers legs hanging down over her shoulders, suspenders dangling.

"Go right into the parlor, and I'll call Aurora down, Miss Delorme. So glad you came of your own accord," declared Mrs. Differdale, somewhat ambiguously I thought, "without waiting for a formal invitation. I did have some ironing to do, but perhaps it will be much better for me to sit here with you and chat. I can iron tonight. Oh, I forgot, there's the sociable. Well, tomorrow, will have to do," she said graciously.

I hated to sit down, after what seemed to me hardly a cordial welcome.

"I'm really in a great hurry," I prevaricated. "I just ran in to see if you could advise me what church is nearest here, and what denomination it is."

"There's a Lutheran church three blocks away: that's the nearest. But I don't think you'd enjoy the preacher, really: he's egotistical. When people give him clever suggestions about building up membership and so forth, he quite scorns them. Then there's a Presbyterian church five blocks up the boulevard. Aurora and I go there. We find the people very congenial, and so appreciative of our efforts to build up the church. And our minister is such a nice little chap, not at all above listening to our advice when we try to help him with suggestions. Aurora! Why don't you come down? We might give Miss Delorme a cup of tea."

"I'll be down as soon as I get my hair fixed," called back the younger woman, in a far from agreeable voice.

"Please don't make any tea for me," I murmured, getting to my feet hurriedly. "I must return at once. I really must. I don't want to interrupt your ironing, and I have much to do

Mrs. Differdale did not try to detain me.

"I know just how that is," she said with a very discernible effort to be agreeable. "I won't detain you, of course." Then with a sudden lowering of her voice: "Did you hear about the Princess Tchemova's five wolves?"

"Oh, are there five!" I murmured.

"Five great savage wolves," affirmed Mrs. Differdale, the soiled boudoir cap bobbing in asseveration. "And the quantities of meat they consume is simply unbelievable. One might almost suspect that the whole household ate nothing but meat," she finished with gusto, her eyes rolling.

"I believe Gus Stieger is pleased with his new customer," I offered, lightly.

"Naturally, Miss Delorme. But if she weren't keeping those wolves well penned up in a strong cage on her grounds, one would feel nervous about having such a menagerie in the neighborhood. They must be frightful, ferocious beasts," she shuddered.

Just as we reached the front hall, Mrs. Arnold came down the stairs. She had removed the white curlpapers and her unnaturally crimped hair lay in ropy locks across her forehead. A sweater of brilliant rose-color concealed part of a not especially fresh blouse.

"I met the princess this morning, mother," said Aurora, with an affected air. "She's really very charming. I had both girls with me, and she admired them so much. She says she simply adores children, and begged me to let her have them over to spend an afternoon with her when she's settled. She was so attracted to Minna. But she told me that she thought Alice needed a more fattening diet, that the child was growing too fast and getting too thin. She is certainly a delightful person," declared Aurora, with a genteel simper.

"She said she wanted us to be over to tea sometime, didn't she, Aurora?" Mrs. Differdale added, with a poorly done attempt at indifference. I could just feel her sense of importance at having thus been singled out of the entire community for this signal honor.

"How lovely!" I said hypocritically, and made my escape with difficulty after all, for both women pursued me out on to the piazza, talking about the Princess Tchemova's beauty, her charm, her wealth, her poise, the social importance of her settling upon Meadowlawn as a place of permanent residence.

As I turned up Gilman Street on my way home, I saw the princess' limousine standing outside Owen's little office, the chauffeur muffled almost to the eyes in shaggy gray fur.

I had sufficient curiosity—perhaps on account of my interest in Owen, for Portia's sake—to walk past the office before crossing. I glanced at the chauffeur as I went by, and was simply aghast at the fierceness of his black eyes; he looked to be a veritable Tartar; as he started unseeingly past me into Owen's office, where the princess sat comfortable enough in a chair never the flat-top desk behind which Owen was ensconced.

The Russian leaned forward, plucking at the same time something from the bosom of her dress. She stretched out slim white arms from the ermine wrap that swathed her lissome figure, and I distinctly saw her fasten something to Owen's coat lapel. It made me feel furious again on Portia's account.

I crossed the road, in front of the limousine. The chauffeur's inscrutable black eyes snapped with such ferocity at the pretty little scene that I actually jumped when he ground out—so explosively, with such concentrated fury that it sent cold chills down my spinal column—what sounded like *"Volko Dlak!"* The sounds stuck so tenuously in my memory that when I got into the house (about past four it was, then) and met Portia, dressed in one of her lovely, clinging, colorful negligees, I asked her at once what the words could be, and articulated them painstakingly for her.

She stared at me for a moment, uncomprehending. Then the soft color began to fade out of her cheeks.

"Not two words, just one," she said, her smooth brow contracting, a strained expression on her face that had ground strangely serious. "I'm afraid that what he said was '*volkod-lak*'."

"You seem to recognize the word phonetically, Portia. Was it Russian? I didn't know you were acquainted with that tongue."

"It was Russian, Aunt Sophie. No, I'm not particularly up in that language, except in the case of a few words, or combinations of words, which I've had occasion to learn during my work with Mr. Differdale. That particular word I know. I wish it had been anything else," she finished somberly. "Don't ask me about it just now, please, Auntie. I'm in no mood to discuss Russian or any other language. But I would like to know just why that chauffer said that," she finished, musingly.

"It's my opinion that he was fearfully upset about something," I contributed. "Do you suppose that he was disgusted to be kept waiting there while milady pinned flowers in Owen's buttonhole?"

There! The cat was out of the bag. I hadn't intended to bother Portia with that, but it just slipped out, inadvertently. I could have bitten off my tongue when she turned her slow gaze upon me as if to verify with her eyes what her ears had heard.

"The Princess Tchernova was pinning a flower on Owen's coat? You saw that? Oh, it is infamous! And I must stand by and do nothing!" burst out my niece. Her feeling seemed to me all out of proportion to the offence. "Yet—I must save him somehow."

She wrung her hands tensely, then with a sudden change of front, took a strong grip on herself and laughed, albeit rather an apology of a laugh.

"Let's have dinner, Aunt Sophie. I think perhaps I worked too late last night and didn't sleep enough today. It's made me irritable. A brisk walk with Boris and Andrei will do me good tonight, after dinner—wake me up a bit, perhaps."

"Oh, Portia, you're not going to work again tonight?" I began, when she silenced me with a single high look.

"Aunt Sophie, when the Bible told us to watch and pray, it should have added, and *work*, lest we fall into the clutches of such foul evil as the human brain can hardly conceive. Come, let's have dinner. Fu must have it ready."

We ate in almost complete silence. I could see that my niece was more than ordinarily abstracted, so I did not try to make conversation, merely replying to such queries as she put to me from time to time.

"What kind of flower was it that the princess pinned on Owen?"

I did not know. I had been far too away to see what it was. And then, while I searched my store of subjective impressions, I remembered that I had seen in the limousine, in passing, a vase of full-blown yellow marigolds.

Portia appeared disturbed again, out of all proportion, when I told her my impression, remarking that I didn't understand how an aristocratic woman like the princess could bear the acrid, pungent odor of those old-fashioned flowers, which are all very well for decorative purposes in flowerbeds, but hardly sweet-perfumed enough for a fastidious woman's taste.

"I mustn't lose my grip on myself. I mustn't. I mustn't," Porta repeated several times.

I thought she must be very tired indeed to let such a trivial incident trouble her so deeply, but laid it to her love for Owen and her fear of losing him.

V

After dinner my niece told me she was going to put on outdoor clothes and I had better change into something darker than the light-gray tailored suit I had worn with my fox-furs that afternoon. When she came into my room, she wore riding breeches under a three-quarters rough tweed overcoat. Boris and Andrei leapt repeatedly upon her, overjoyed with the prospect of an outside run, which they understood they were to have when they saw leashes and a short whip in their mistress' leather-gauntleted hands.

"Will you take Boris, Aunt Sophie? Boris is easier to manage, I think. You'd best take the whip too. I shan't need it with Andrei. In fact, I shouldn't need it at all, both dogs are so accustomed to immediate obedience to my voice. You may possibly be obliged to use it as a persuasive for Boris, who isn't entirely used to you yet."

She leashed the hounds and gave Boris over to me, and we went out into the quiet night. The plan was to walk up Gilman Street in the opposite direction from Queen Boulevard, and return past the old Burnham house.

Portia seemed worked up about something. I presumed she was still thinking about the Russian and the flower in Owen's buttonhole, so I remained silent rather than to appear cognizant of her thoughts. Presently, however, as we turned to the left, I asked her if we had any special objective, apart from walking past the Burnham house. I could feel her eyes upon me in the soft darkness.

"We're going to take a little walk about the Burnham grounds, Aunt Sophie. I want to see—I want—oh, it's very hard to explain! You may think it dreadful of me—but—Auntie, you've just got to trust me, that's all. I've got to go into the princess' grounds. I've got to look into her windows, if I get a chance. I can't explain everything now, but my reason is very important, more than I can possibly tell you. Won't you trust me, please?"

Her voice was so entreating that I felt my heart pushing the words of assent to my tongue's tip. After all, Portia was my niece. She cared for Own Edwardes. I really could not believe that the Russian, so exotic and bizarre a creature, could have become in reality, fascinated by a young man who was, after all, just a good-looking, healthy, young American businessman. If the princess did not care for him, then she only wanted to flirt, to pass away some idle moments in what to her was only a pastime. I ranged myself on Portia's side immediately, feeling that my niece was being urged by some motive bigger than mere feminine jealousy, and that she would make this clear to me in good time.

"Portia, my dear, you do just what you think is best. I can't say I'm especially attracted to the princess. And," I added, my heart suddenly warming pleasantly at the sudden recollection, "I like the way Owen calls me Aunt Sophie!"

Portia came close to my side, reached out her free hand, and gave my arm a caress that meant more than words. I felt that she understood what a strong ally she had in Sophie Delorme.

By the time we reached the grounds of the princess' house, the dogs had quieted down a little from the exuberant spirits they had shown during the first part of our walk, when they had pulled at their leashes wildly. It may be have been fancy, but I felt that Boris showed distinct reluctance to enter the grounds of the Russian's house, grounds full of deep, dark shadows from the shrubbery that would be so beautiful in the summer but that now seemed terrifyingly like hideous, ragged-garbed skeletons in the dim-light of the stars.

"Auntie," whispered my niece guardedly, although we were far enough from the house to have spoken loudly without having been overheard, "will you take Andrei's leash, please, and wait for me here? I'm going into the grounds and I can see that the dogs won't be pleased to accompany me."

"I don't want you to go alone," I whispered back, suddenly oppressed with a disinclination to remain there myself alone, where every bush seemed a skulking beast ready to spring out upon me. I was ashamed, but I preferred going with Portia into I knew not what, to remaining alone.

"Well, we can try it with the dogs, but I'm afraid they won't come, Aunt Sophie."

We experience no particular trouble, however. Keeping close to the hedge that bordered the path to the rear of the house, Portia and I walked cautiously along with Boris and Andrei held tightly and close to us, until we had reached the house. There were lights in front, and I felt Portia's hand drawing me in the direction of the drawing room windows. We managed to get behind a great scrawny bush that scattered the light streaming from one as yet uncurtained French window (I have since wondered at the carelessness of the princess that night in exposing her intimate home life to the curious eye of the midnight prowler. At any rate, the following day, curtains hung at all windows and were drawn at dusk).

THE SCENE WITHIN THE GREAT drawing room was a lively one. The princess glittering and shimmering in a gown of some clinging green metallic cloth, reclined on a heap of what appeared to be rich rugs thrown over piled cushions. A band of gold set with diamonds flashed about her head and from it hung a square diamond by a link, so that it flashed with dazzling rainbow splendor as she turned her head from side to side. Her garment clung about her as if they had been molded to her supple form and were indeed a part of her own personality.

She was evidently directing the arrangement of draperies and furniture in her new home. As she directed, long white arms and pointed fingers glittering with flashing gems, the chauffeur and a bent old woman hurried hither and thither to carry out her orders.

The chauffeur was a handsome fellow in a heavy way, and apparently deeply attached to his mistress, to judge from the solicitous manner in which he carried out her commands.

The woman (I learned later that her name was Agathya) was much older than her mistress, who might have been any age from sixteen to forty, so vivid and strange was her exotic loveliness. Agathya looked about sixty. She had straggling gray hair, drawn tightly back into a bunch at the top of her head. Her face was deeply lined, her eyes roving, her manner shrinking and servile. She wore a dark brown one-piece dress, gridled by a brown silk cord, and was barefooted. Her stooped shoulders made her appear of medium height, but I think Agathya would have been a tall woman had she thrown back her shoulders and stood upright.

These two people approached their mistress with attitudes so entirely different that it was like watching a drama on a stage to look through that wide window and see them; the man with a proud kind of watchful anxiety to please, the woman seemingly half terrorized, trembling and shrinking everytime the princess addressed her.

"Portia, I believe that poor old woman is ill-treated," I whispered, as we saw Agathya shrink backward at a sudden motion of the Russian's hand toward her.

I had hardly said it before something happened in the lighted room. The old woman, attempting to place a vase upon the tall mantel shelf, miscalculated, slipped, and to save herself let the vase go. It fell, crashing, to the tiled hearth. Agathya did not rise from the crumpled, shrunken heap into which she had huddled her body.

The princess Irma rose, however. She flew out of the pile of cushions, her face transformed by fury. She ran over to that prostrate figure coruching there. She stood over it for a moment, saying something that we could not hear, nor could we have understood her Russian had we heard. Then she thrust out a small foot shod with a buckled shoe, the heel of which sparkled with brilliants, and gave that poor old woman's form a harsh push that sent Agathya sliding across the hearth. Nor did it end here. The Russian snatched at something that had been lying on the mantel, and lifted one arm high over the poor creature who now began to struggle upward, with lifted hands and arms over her face.

From my reading I recognized the instrument that the princess wielded as a knout, and felt sick at what was apparently about to happen. But the man came springing across the room to her side. He leaned down with careless indifference to the princess' rage and helped Agatha to her feet. Then he turned and began to talk to his mistress, who listened with head thrown back, eyes flashing redly upon him. Her arm dropped; she let the knout slip from her jeweled fingers, and laughed. Her begemmed hand motioned away Agathya, who slunk from the room, head bowed, shoulders bent, like one mortal fear.

"Sergei! Sergei!" I could hear the princess cry out clearly, between trills of gurgling laughter that I rather saw than heard. She put out her hand to him, with an inimitably gracious gesture, and he caught it to his lips, sinking to one knee as he kissed it with passionate abandon. She withdrew it then, with a kind of indifference, leaned over, passed her cheek lightly across his upturned, adoring face. At that, he flung himself flat upon the rugs at her feet, and I could see that he was putting her dress to his lips as he almost groveled there.

So quick had been the little drama that neither Portia nor I had a chance to interchange a word, but now Portia pulled at me, and I wakened to the realization that it was not my niece alone who was drawing me from the vicinity of the lighted window, but Boris, who tugged at his leash, whimpering softly. I let myself be drawn away, and followed Portia until we emerged from the path that led to Queens Boulevard, down which we went in the direction of home.

"The man's mad over her!" exploded Portia, as we regained the boulevard. "Now I can account for his exclamation. He was furious with jealously, and his position as her chauffeur restrained him from interrupting her flirtation with Owen. In that moment, he had forgot himself and said what he would not have breathed, had he known that you had such a keen car and such a good memory. Oh, I begin to see! I begin to understand!"

"The poor old woman!" I exclaimed indignantly. "Why does she remain with such a cruel mistress?"

"A serf, perhaps. Or an old nurse. Such a woman will bear all kinds of abuse from the mistress who was once a child she nurtured at her breast," explained Portia.

Just then we passed the lower end of the princess' grounds, and both dogs began behaving uneasily. Boris pulled and twisted at his leash so that I had hard work to hold him in; Anderi sniffed and whined.

"I wonder—" murmured Portia. Then, as if with a sudden thought that did not affect her agreeable, she said in a low, cautiously modulated voice, "The quicker we get home the better. The dogs are so uneasy that it disturbs me. Suppose that cage of wolves happened to be less strong that I hope it is?"

The supposition certainly was one to lend wings to our feet. I said immediately, "Let's run Portia!"

"Can you?" answered she, as if gratified, "Come on, then!"

The dogs pulled us strongly toward home, the moment they found we were going to race them. We passed the Burnham house grounds at a run and went tearing along the boulevard toward Gilman Street in a way that surely would have ruined any reputation for dignity either of us might have hoped to sustain in the neighborhood, had we been seen. Fortunately, we met no one, the night being very crisp and sharp. Too, we kept to the farther side of the street from the lamps, which are in front of the store-block only, the other side of the boulevard being as yet nothing but wide fields, except for the Burnham house.

We reached home out of breath; even the dogs were panting hard. After Portia unleashed them, they seemed quite contended to walk sedately beside us when we went up to our rooms, instead of leaping up playfully as they usually did.

Boris insisted upon sleeping on the fur rug in my room that night; perhaps because he felt we were better acquainted after our long run together that evening. As for Anderi, he accompanied Portia to her room, where both dogs usually sleep nightly on a rug before her door. She left him there, and half an hour later passed my door on her way to the laborator, wearing a black silk bungalow apron, I should call it, with a girdle of silk cord. Portia called it her working uniform.

My sleep was broken that night. Twice I waked with the uncomfortable feeling that I was not alone in the room, and turned on the electric light quickly to find nothing but the dog, which lifted wide open eyes to me. It was as if some malign influence had come with me from the old Burnham house. I think Portia looked upon it from another standpoint, for when I mentioned it to her at lunch she looked rather serious and observed that she really shouldn't have exposed me to those influences without preparation. Evidently she was of the opinion that I was open to psychic powers that had either followed me from the princess' house, or had escaped from Portia's magical circles in the courtyard! I laughed at her solemnly, but her grave expression was rather disquieting.

"There's a great deal going on that I cannot explain to you just now, Auntie," she said earnestly. "I hope that the necessity for explanation will never come, but I fear my hope is vain."

Fu Sing came rather hurriedly into the room as we were rising from the table, with the information that Mr. Edwardes was on the wire. There was an extension in the hall just off the dining room and I could hear my niece's voice distinctly.

"Yes, this is Portia Differdale. Oh, yes, Owen. What? My dogs loose last night? Impossible! What? The princess saw them? Really, Owen, I—I don't know what to say. Aunt Sophie and I had both dogs out with us last night, on the leash, and we didn't let them away from us once."

All at once her voice sounded pleading.

"Owen, as a favor to me, please don't mention that my dogs were out last night. Deny it, please, in my name. I—I have a special reason for my request. Thank you, my dear friend."

She rang off and came to rejoin me in the dining room. Her eyes were alight with the fire of purpose. Her whole bearing had become invested with a dignity, a force, that reminded me of the tone of some of her letters to me after her marriage with Mr. Differdale.

"Aunt Sophie, the Princess Tchernova has been complaining that two immense white wolfhounds were loose on her grounds last night, trying to worry her wolves in the wolfden at the foot of her grounds."

"Impossible that she could have seen us, Portia!"

"It matters little how she knew, Aunt Sophie. I am persuaded that her selecting last night to complain of my dogs is merely a coincidence, and that she has made the accusation to cover up something, to afford and excuse for some trick she is contemplating—what, I can only imagine, and my imagination is playing me unholy tricks this morning," my niece said thoughtfully.

"But what good could it possibly do to have it known that Boris and Andrei were loose last night in her grounds?" I persisted, very much puzzled.

"I can surmise, Auntie, but I cannot make my surmises public at this stage. It's hard to do so, but I must wait until—until something happens."

There was in Portia's voice, a strange note that trouble me vaguely, yet it was nothing upon which I could put my finger, so to speak.

"One thing I must ask of you, Aunt Sophie, and that is that you keep within the walls of this place after dusk. I'm not asking this for a whim, but out of my knowledge of a terrible danger that I am now persuaded lurks about us; that is crouching, ready to spring out upon us at the moment when we least suspect it."

"I presume you will remain inside yourself, then?" I inquired, naturally enough.

"If I can mange to do so, I will," she rejoined. "Do not forget that I have learned much since I lived with you in Reading, Auntie. There are certain potent influences, certain natural laws, upon which I can depend for my protection by my knowledge of them, and hence my power over them. But there—I see that you do not in the least understand me."

"I must say you are talking in riddles, my dear Portia."

"I see that I must speak plainly. There is a certain mighty power for evil that has taken up its residence in Meadowlawn. I hesitate to name it, but it is, nevertheless, here in this community. I know how to protect myself against it, but you do not. Therefore you must remain within these walls after nightfall."

I was somewhat provoked at Portia's rather high-handed order, as I have walked alone through the loneliest parts of Reading outskirts, unaccomplished.

"If you are so anxious about me, how about Owen?" I inquired, a bit maliciously, I admit.

"Oh!" She expelled her breath sharply. "Owen I am powerless to protect! I cannot give an order to him as I can to you, Auntie. He would want to know my reasons, and I'm sure he would laugh at them when he knew them, because he couldn't understand."

Ingenuous girl, thought I to myself, how little she really knew me, if she thought I would let myself be ordered about in that manner. I made up my mind that she was letting her imagination run away with her. I intended to go to the Sunday evening service at the end of the week, and I certainly did not expect to ask for an escort of policemen to accompany me, because my niece was nervous and (perhaps) notional.

VI

The balance of the week passed quietly enough. Portia devoted herself again to her laboratory work night. I did my marketing daily, occasionally running into Mrs. Differdale or Mrs. Arnold, almost invariably with their hair done up in curl-papers over which they airily wore their soiled satin boudoir caps.

Mrs. Arnold kept me fifteen minutes at Mike's one morning, telling me that Minna had been very sick with a bilious attack from eating too much candy. She retailed all Minna's symptoms; her own prompt use of the clinical thermometer; the doctor's report; Minna's recovery; ending with the remark that the next time the Princess Irma gave Minna chocolates, she (Aurora) had ordered Minna to bring them home and not try to eat all at one sitting. I received the impression, somehow, that had Minna been of a less fine and delicate constitution, she would not have been affected by the sweets, Aurora remarking that Minna was, like herself, as high-strung as a violin, this simile appearing to afford her much innocent satisfaction, as placing her on a higher plane than the rest of us vulgarly healthy mortals.

Sunday morning I told Portia that I intended to go to the evening service. She looked simply aghast.

"But I thought I explained to you," she began, when I interrupted her.

"My dear Portia, at my age I don't intend to be dictated to as to what hours I shall appear on the street. Curfew empathetically does *not* ring for me, my dear girl. If you're worrying about the Princess Tchernova's wolves, I may as well tell you that yesterday Owen took me into the grounds to show me the wolfdens of cement and steel that she has had built, and they're quite strong enough to keep the animals inside."

Portia stared at me, her face disturbed by some deep emotion.

"I'll go with you," she suddenly decided.

"By no means interrupt your laboratory work," I retorted. "You know church services always did bore you to extinction. I won't have you going on my account."

Portia did not answer me, but I felt that she would do or say something to prevent me, and was agreeably surprised that she did not attempt to dissuade me at seven o'clock, when I looked into the library to bid her goodbye. On the contrary, she was dressed in knickers and tweed coat, and the dogs were leashed, the leashes slipped over her left wrist. In her right hand she help the whip she had given to me to carry a few nights before.

"I'm going to walk along with you, if you don't mind. I won't go in," she said.

I couldn't very well object, so she and Boris and Andrei went along up Queens Boulevard with me, very much to the astonishment of other churchgoing people, of whom not a few were on their way in my direction. I mentioned this to Portia, but she acted rather sulkily for her, and continued to walk along beside me. As we passed the police station—a little boxlike shanty opposite Mike's store on the boulevard—O'Brien came out and cross the road towards us.

"Good evenin', ma'am. Did I see one of your dogs over in the Burnham house grounds last night?" he asked.

Portia straightened up and met his eyes determinedly.

"Neither last night, nor any other night, officer. I keep my dogs on the leash when they're out, and when they're not with me in the street, they're inside ten-foot walls. It was not one of my dogs you saw, I can assure you."

Her voice became hard and tense then.

"If I were you, I'd keep an eye on those wolves. Is there—is there a white one among them, perhaps?"

Her insinuation was entirely lost on O'Brien. Still, he looked at Boris and Andrei as if he would have liked to put the blame of whatever he had seen upon them. Then he went back across the road.

Portia was more than ever grave after this snatch of conversation.

"Do you see, Aunt Sophie, how the princess is trying to shift blame for something upon my noble dogs? I suppose you don't understand yet why I am accompanying you? I hope you'll never have to learn the real reason," she ended sadly.

"I think you might be doing a sensible thing to take your aunt into your confidence, Portia Delorme." I responded heatedly. "I'm sorry, but I fear it is a very small and petty feeling on your part that makes so prejudiced against the Princess Tchernova. She may be cruel and flirt, but I hardly believe that she is laying deep plans to get a couple of innocent dogs in trouble."

I couldn't help laughing. Portia tightened her lips and did not speak again, until she said goodbye at the church steps.

WHEN I CAME OUT AFTER the service I attached myself to the Arnolds. Aurora having attended with her husband. As we came down the boulevard, we became aware that something of an alarming nature had undoubtedly happened in the vicinity of the stores. There were many people buzzing about, the crowd seeming to center near the drugstore on the corner. Mr. Arnold left us and penetrated the crowd, returning after a minute with exciting news.

Officer O'Brien had been attracted by some large white animal that looked over the hedge of the Burnham place. He went over to investigate, loosening his revolver in case of emergency. It was the firing of his revolver that had attracted people to his rescue, among them Portia Differdale, with her two wolfhounds, which she had loosed from their leashes (when Mr. Arnold said this, his wife pursed her lips with a significant look and remarked that those dogs were savage beasts that would some day attach her or somebody else). Boris and Andrei had last been seen disappearing into the dark of the Burnham grounds, in pursuit, so Portia declared, of the beast that had so badly torn and clawed the arm and shoulder of the policeman.

Not for a single minute did I believe that those dogs had been guilty of attacking O'Brien, but I could see how the people around considered the matter. In public opinion, Boris and Andrei had already been tried and condemned. It made me furious. I pushed my way into the drugstore, although they tried to hold me back, for I was determined to get at Portia. I could see her kneeling by the man's side, bandaging his arm and shoulder, and the smell of iodoform filled the night air.

Presently she stood up, just as I centered the pharmacy. I thought for a moment that I saw a fleeting reproach in her eyes, and I remembered that it was my insistence upon going to church that had brought Portia out with the dogs.

"There's nothing else to be done but send him to the hospital when the ambulance comes," I heard her saying to Dietz, the druggist. "When the relieving officer arrives and starts investigations, I wish it to be given as my statement that my two dogs were leashed securely and I only gave them their freedom after I heard the shot, because I wanted to send them to O'Brien's assistance."

Her eyes, cold and stern, passed over the faces of the listeners, who stopped their whispering until she had passed through the crowd. She joined me at the door. We went off down the boulevard together, Portia occasionally whistling to summon the dogs, which dashed up to us just as we turned off the boulevard. I must say that I felt somehow very glad of the protection of those stanch beasts; if I were to take Portia's word and the officer's experience, then there was a third white dog abroad, not an entirely agreeable dog to meet, judging from the badly chewed left arm and shoulder of O'Brien.

We reached home without further incident. Portia let the dogs loose in the enclosure about the house and herself went down at once into the laboratory, with an implacable, set expression on her face that impressed me she knew more than she chose to tell about the happenings of the evening.

Next morning a policeman named O'Toole came to the house to interview Portia as to her share in the evening's happening. He took down her simple and direct statement without comment, but he did seem (I was present, to confirm Portia's statement as to her reason for being abroad with the dogs) vastly interested in the great ten-foot wall and in the immense courtyard with is circles and strange symbols cut into the cement paving. He was tactful enough to say nothing, although his eyes roved everywhere. I had a feeling that his reports to interested inquirers in the community would stimulate interest and speculation yet further about the Differdale house. I could almost hear him saying: "Nary a chair. Nothing but cushions to sit on."

MRS. DIFFERDALE CALLED ME ON THE telephone about eleven o'clock to ask if I wouldn't drop in for tea that afternoon about half past three; she said she was having somebody else whom she thought I'd enjoy meeting. I really had no good excuse to offer, and on second thought it occurred to me that it might be as well to go, in order to put in a good word for the dogs. I was morally certain that I was being asked to satisfy the curiosity of those two women. I asked Fu to tell his mistress where I'd gone (Portia did not appear at luncheon) and left the house about three o'clock.

Owen Edwardes was not in his office when I passed. I wondered if he were also out at tea that afternoon, perhaps with the Princess Tchernova. As I turned up Elm Street, a limousine flashed past me, and stopped before the Arnold house. A moment later the sinuous form of the Russian stepped out of the shining car and mounted the house steps. Then it flashed across me whom it was Mrs. Differdale had meant by someone I'd enjoy meeting.

I felt angry. I had been trapped into meeting a woman who was striking underhanded blows at Portia, trapped into meeting her in a friendly, social way. I hesitated, I was half of a mind to turn back.

And then it was too late, for Mrs. Differdale, opening the door to the princess with a gushing greeting which the Russian acknowledged with her inscrutable smile, saw me and called my name. I could not very well get out of it, so I went forward with what grace I could summon on such short notice.

"Ah, it is the dear Ow-een's Aunt Sophie! *Chère* Aunt Sophie, in this wilderness how *charmant* to meet a soul kindred soul!"

She turned to her hostess, a pointed pink tongue moistening her lips with a lapping motion, that unpleasant little habit of hers to which Portia had referred.

"You are a good creature to have prepare this so beautiful surprise for me, *chère amie. But let us go in; the spring air is not yet so warm.*"

Her trailing metallic silks made it necessary for me to maintain a respectful distance from her, for which I was not sorry. It certainly seemed that in a moment she would have put her slender arms about me, have touched my cheeks with her red lips, such did her enthusiasm appear to be over our meeting. I could not help being a little flattered; after all, I am but human, and even if I did dislike her, why should I be displeased because she tried to be nice to me?

The two Arnold girls, Minna and Alice, had been dressed in white dresses for the grand occasion, and stood with beribboned hair, waiting for the company to arrive. Minna evidently felt very much at home with the princess, for she immediately went forward with the assurance of a favorite, and seated herself beside the charming Russian who put an arm about the girl, pinching the plump shoulders playfully.

"*So you were sick eating my chocolates, Minna? Pauvre enfant!* Another time we must not eat so much at one time. But the sweets are good for you, little one; they will make you as round and plump as a fat patridge!"

The princess' laugh rang out merrily at her comparison. Minna laughed, also, but even in her pert pride at having been singled out by the princess, the child did not forget to give me a saucy look. She certainly was a disagreeable child; there is no doubt about that.

"It is a pity Minna didn't share her chocolates with Alice," put in Mrs. Arnold, who wore the dress she had worn to the Sunday evening service, a homemade black velvet with a lace collar that was the only redeeming feature of the garment. "Alice needs to put on flesh far more than Minna."

"You are right, *chère* Mrs. Arnold."

The princess turned her attention to Alice.

"It shall be the little sister who shall have the next boxful of bonbons."

The pointed little white teeth showed in a smile that for some reason did not give me pleasure. Instead, I felt as if something unbenign lay hidden behind the Princess Tchernova's apparent interest in the two children. I wondered if her own impulsive, cruel nature, as I had seen it illustrated that other evening when she thought herself unobserved, drew her to the two children, children disliked by everyone on the street and in the neighborhood for their bad dispositions.

"Minna shall come to my house this evening," purred the princess, "and I shall have for her a very big box of sweets, but she must give half of them to Alice."

Minna laughed throatily and threw a self-conscious look at me.

"I can't come Princess Tchernova"—(her childish tongue tripped over that outlandish name)—"because my Aunt Portia's big dogs might bite me the way they did O'Brien."

"*Mr.* O'Brien, darling," corrected her mother primly.

"Your Aunt Portia's dogs *didn't* bite *Mr.* O'Brien," I put in at this point, determined not to let that story go any further if I could prevent it.

"Oh, *chère* Aunt Sophie, what a loyal heart is yours!" sighed the Russian, turning those green shining eyes full upon me. "How nobly you try to shield the savage beasts of Mrs. Differdale! But why?"

"Why, princess? Because I've had Boris out with me on the leash and I've seen both dogs around the house everyday. They sleep in my room or Portia's half the time. They're as gentle as babies and as sweet-dispositioned," I retorted.

"But then," hesitated she prettily, again with that pointed tongue lapping her deep red lips, "you must know Mrs. Differdale very well indeed, that she let you enter her so-mysterious home of many secrets. I thought you were the Aunt Sophie of my Ow-een!"

There! How was that for sheer nerve on her part? She rested her green eyes on me with a kind of amused smile flickering over her dead-white face, a smile that said much to the contrary of what her lips uttered.

"I am Mrs. Differdale's aunt, her father's sister," said I pointedly. "And I consider myself in a position to deny spiteful rumors about such magnificent beasts as Boris and Andrei."

"The aunt of the mysterious Mrs. Differdale? A-ah, that explains everything! *Vraiment!*"

She brushed away my denial, my explanation, with a little wave of her gemmed fingers. I was furious, but there was nothing more for me to say at the moment. I took the cup of tea Mrs. Arnold offered, and sipped it hurriedly. I like my tea with sugar and lemon, and my hostess had asked if I wanted cream.

When they asked the princess she cried at once: "No sugar, please! I do not like sweet things. Sweet things are for dear little plump girl. The plain tea, please, without anything."

"No sugar? No milk?" cried Aurora.

"Cream," corrected the mother in an undertone, looked up, caught my eye and colored.

"Nothing, kind friends, but the plain tea. No thank you, no cakes. The doctor, he do not permit sweet cakes for the poor Irma, who must do what she is order."

I made a mental note of these preferences and dislikes, thinking that it might interest Portia, who seemed to find such weighty matter in my most trifling reports.

The Russian had removed her ermine cap and it now lay on her silken knees. The ermine cloak was thrown open, displaying the silken clinging draperies of her gown, which was girdled with a wide belt set with square diamonds surrounded with colored jewels in a barbaric and striking design. About her forehead was bound the golden ribbon I had seen that other night; the square-cut diamond twinkled and winked evilly at her every motion. Frightfully had taste for the simple occasion, but undeniably gorgeous and attractive.

The doorbell rang and Mrs. Differdale, throwing me a peculiar look, went to answer it. I heard and recognized a man's voice.

"Here's the copy of that deed, Mrs. Differdale. I rushed it through just as quickly as I could, to get it to you this afternoon as you wished."

"Do come in and have a cup of tea," urged she. "Miss Delorme's here."

"That is an inducement. Of course, I'll have a cup of tea, if I can drink it with her," laughed Owen, parting the portieres and smiling down upon us.

"Ah, *cher ami*," cried the princess, extending a jeweled hand and monopolizing Owen entirely, so that all he could do was to bow and smile at me across the room, "what a pleasure is this so unexpected meeting, to drink the friendly tea with you in the home of these so kind ones!"

She caressed the two women with her green, glowing eyes, then turned her gaze full upon me.

"What, Ow-een? You do not pay to the Aunt Sophie your respects? Bad man! Go, at once, on the command of Irma Andreyevna Tchernova, and kneel at the feet of Aunt Sophie!"

Owen took immediate advantage of the order, which the Russian flavored with a peculiar smile at me, a smile tinctured with irony and that confidence in her own entire command of the situation that is so exasperating from one woman to another.

Mrs. Differdale poured a cup of tea for the newcomer, and I caught an interchange of glances between her daughter and herself.

"I would have invited my sister-in-law, Miss Delorme, but one doesn't exactly care to be snubbed more than two or three times." suddenly burst out Mrs. Arnold with a vehemence that spoke of her having only wailed a fitting time to explode her bottled-up indignation. "Portia is so odd about going out socially," and she shrugged her shoulders expressively, if inelegantly, under the clumsy velvet.

"Oh, I'm sure Portia—Mrs. Differdale—" hastily corrected Owen, coming to the defense of the absent accused with a warmth that did my heart good, "wouldn't dream of snubbing anybody, least of all her late husband's people."

"How kind are the thoughts of Ow-een!" murmured the guest of honor, an expression of deep admiration on her oval face. "Always he wishes to think the best about everybody. Ah, we are not all so noble," sighed she. For some reason, her green eyes still sought my face.

Illogical on my part, if you will, but I could have slapped the princess: her inference was by far too plain to be ignored by a friend of Portia's. I jumped boldly into the fray.

"My niece is one of the kindest-hearted. noblest women I ever had the privilege of knowing, Mrs. Arnold. She would never dream of snubbing anybody. I'm sure you've misinterpreted her unwillingness to leave her work, to which she is absolutely devoted."

"What work can possibly keep a woman as occupied as Portia, so that she never goes out socially, dear Miss Delorme? I've tried to let my daughter-in-law know that she's being frightfully gossiped about, staying in that great house all alone, doing Lord knows what."

"Whatever Mrs. Differdale is occupied in doing must be of a splendid and worthwhile nature. Anybody who has the honor of her acquaintance knows that," broke in Owen.

He glanced quickly about the little circle and caught the subtly ironical smile of the Russian. I could see that be was slightly disconcerted by it.

"Ow-een, we must all believe you too much interest in the mysterious lady, if you defend her so warmly," accused Irma, shaking an index finger at him merrily.

Owen colored deeply. It was a betrayal for those who were able to read the signs, but I do not think anyone but myself and the argus-eyed princess translated that blush. Irma Tchernova did not appear pleased, for through her parted lips I could see those white teeth set tightly together.

"Mr. Edwardes is quite right, princess, to defend my niece, exactly as I did. When you know her better, you will jump to her defense at the first word of criticism," I exclaimed in quick refutal of the Russian's innuendo.

She turned her head ever so slowly, until her long, narrow eyes were full upon me. In the growing dusk it seemed to me that red light glinted across the oriental-looking orbs, and it disturbed me, affecting me most disagreeably. I was glad when the Alice, who suddenly thrust out one hand and made a snatch at the bonbons on the tea table.

Her mother slapped at the child's wrist, so that the candy tumbled helter-skelter over the embroidered teacloth and upon the carpet. It was the princess who intervened, her attention drawn from me to the miniature battle between mother and daughter.

"Oh, dear Mrs. Arnold, do let Alice have the bonbons! She love them so," cooed she. "And she is so thin, poor little one. If she were only like her sister, how glad I should be! But then, if she eat many bonbons, perhaps she will sometime be round and rosy, eh, Alice?"

She finished by taking a handful of the candy and filling the outstretched hands of Alice, who smirked her triumph. (Odious child! I cannot help it, even today.)

I had finished my second cup of tea by this time, and felt no inclination to remain longer. I rose to my feet and observed that I had promised to be home by five o'clock. Owen stood up at once and offered to accompany me, if I would allow him. Then the princess interfered, with honeyed sweetness that sickened me with an intuition of her depths of deception, for I was not deceived; I knew she did not like me.

"Let me take you both in my car!" she cried with a semblance of spontaneous enthusiasm. "Then, Ow-een, we shall both carry the dear Aunt Sophie to her home, and you shall see that Irma Andreycvna Tchernova is not kidnapped on her way back! Has not Irma the wonderful ideas?"

PART II

I

Part I

THERE WAS NO WAY TO evade the proffered invitation. Owen and I walked behind the trailing-robed, sinuous, triumphant princess, and her savage-eyed chauffeur helped each in turn into her limousine. It made me think of ancient conquerors and their captives of war.

I was thankful that the cut-glass vase did not hold marigolds, the odor of which I detest; it was full on this occasion of lilies-of-the-valley, which had filled the car with an almost cloying sweetness of perfume.

As we rolled down Elm Street toward the boulevard, I leaned forward to examine more closely a central flower in the white-and-green of the valley lilies, a flower that to me was a hideous travesty upon the beauty of nature's garden products. It was of a deep burnt-orange color, with irregular, swollen black blotches, and the petals were not delicately translucent as orchids I have seen mostly were, but of a thick fleshiness that was somehow unpleasantly suggestive of—of life!—Not the innocent life of a flower, but life that reeked of something inherently, powerfully evil and malevolent.

"You admire my beautiful Balkan orchid, yes, Aunt Sophie?" asked the princess, her delicate brows raised slightly as if she herself were not quite sure of the purpose of my extreme interest in the strange-appearing flower.

"I presumed it was an orchid, princess, but I cannot agree with you that it is beautiful. Isn't it responsible for the rather acrid, pungent odor that is mingled with the perfume of the lilies-of-the-valley?" I countered.

The Russian withdrew her eyes, the crimson lips all at once tightening.

"Ah, then you do not like my orchid? So many," caressingly, "do not like it at first and then—afterward—they grow to love it."

I sensed something intangible but none the less sinister in her words.

"Ow-een, you shall show to Aunt Sophie that some of my friends do value my so-wonderful orchid."

She leaned forward, drew out the strange, fleshy-petaled thing, its thick stem oozing a sticky sap, and put it in Owen's buttonhole with a proprietary air. The sickly, faintish odor pervaded the limousine.

Owen laughed, but I fancied that his laugh was not a happy one. He glanced at me in a half-troubled fashion, and I smiled back broadly to express my confidence in him. After all, poor fellow, it wasn't his fault if a lovely woman chose to distinguish him before the aunt of the girl he loved. Then I saw his eyes drop and his brow gather as he regarded the blossom—no, I can't call it that, and I didn't then, even in my own mind—the—*thing*—in his buttonhole.

"Thank you for the flower, princess. I must confess that I agree with Miss Delorme," formally, "that its odor is far from agreeable. I presume you're accustomed to it, aren't you? Perhaps for some sentimental reason?"

"It may be an acquired taste, like olives," I put in.

"My father was very fond of such orchids, Ow-een. He had many house of glass on his estate, full of these—experiment." The princess spoke a bit carefully, her narrowed eyes shifting from Owen's face to mine. "I have but few, yet more wonderful than this one. I have the great blood-red orchid that seem so solid, so yielding, at once—like the pulsing flesh of a child's heart."

I couldn't restrain an exclamation of disgust and horror at the simile, and the princess straightened her slim form suddenly and changed her tone, with a gracious smile.

"And the thick white flower as of new-fallen snow," she purred, "is one of the most lovely. But I see the *chère tante* is not interest in Irma Tchernova's poor flowers," plaintively. "Ah, perhaps, some day you will come, then, to see my jewels? You are a woman and must be interest in the jewels? I have many that are most fine, of the diamond, the ruby, the sapphire, the emerald," she ended, leaning toward me engagingly with what I am sure she intended for a friendly smile.

Such was my interior impression of her exactly opposite feeling toward me that I withdrew almost involuntarily from her advances and she observed this with a slight twitch of her crimson lips. The situation might have become further strained, had we not stopped at that moment before the great wall about the Differdale house.

OWEN SPRANG OUT TO RING the bell, and waited with me beside the door, hoping—I felt so, at least—that Portia might appear when the gate swung open, instead of Fu Sing. Sure enough, she did, and put out her hand to him prettily, to thank him for having brought me home.

"Don't thank me," he said, motioning to the limousine drawn close to the curb. "The Princess Tchernova—oh, you two have already met, haven't you?"

"Why, yes, I think we have met," Portia drawled, her clear eyes upon the glowing garnet eyes of the Russian, who leaned back in the car almost as if she desired to escape notice.

Then her tone changed from indifference to a tense alarm that startled me so much that I leaned back against the open gate, panting at the suddenness of her attack.

"Who gave you this—this *thing*?" demanded my niece sharply, and plucked at Owen's buttonhole as if she were conquering an innate reluctance to touch something horribly loathsome. "Oh, it is not necessary to answer. I know!"

With a quick, nervous jerk she pulled the strange and monstrous bloom from Owen's buttonhole and let it fall upon the ground. Then she put out one foot and crushed it into a pulpy, nasty mass that sent its sharp, acrid, disagreeable odor puffing up into the air about us. At once she seemed to recover herself.

"That—flower—princess, is dangerous. I wonder if you know *how* dangerous?"

Rapierlike glances shot between the two women. "Owen, I didn't mean to startle you," Portia continued, "but that—flower—is a very poisonous—orchid. I'm sure the princess wasn't aware of its bad qualities," and another sharp interchange of glances took place. "I'm sorry, princess, if I spoiled a favorite—flower—of yours. I presume it came from your hothouses?" She directed her remarks to the silent occupant of the limousine. "Of course, you have—others?"

I felt, as I had been feeling when Portia made certain remarks, insignificant in themselves, that they had a deep inner meaning running through and under them. I was convinced that, whatever it was that my niece meant to convey, the Princess Tchernova caught her idea clearly. There was a moment's silence, then the Russian leaned toward the open door of the limousine and spoke slowly, each word dropping like venomous slobbering driblets from a mad beast's jaws, so concentrated was the bad feeling that I knew lay behind each syllable.

"*Ma chère* Mrs. Differdale, I have many—others. Do not fear that I resent or misunderstand your—your uncalculated action. You shall see some day—the many—others." She turned to Owen. "Poisonous? Tchah!" contemptuously.

Then she smiled, such a smile as chilled my very heart, there was such tense purpose in her tight-locked teeth, her narrowed green eyes, as she fixed her gaze upon Portia.

"Are you going on, Owen? Or will you stop in for a moment?"

I was astounded at Portia's invitation, after all our hashing and rehashing of the delicate situation, but laid it to her ill-concealed jealousy of the other woman, who continued to smile without speaking. I could see that Owen wanted to come in, but felt Portia's invitation a trifle tactless under the circumstances.

"Any other time," he began hastily, when he was interrupted by the princess, whose evil smile had never once left her red lips.

"Any other time, *chère* Mrs. Differdale. But Ow-een is promis' to me for now. Are you not, my Ow-een?"

Her assumption of proprietorship was certainly enough to have made any woman furious. Portia whitened and winced.

"Some other time, then, Mr. Edwardes," said she, pointedly, and withdrew inside the bronze doors, motioning me to follow so that she could close them.

Owen was dreadfully disturbed, it was plain to see, but there was nothing for it but for him to bid us good evening and withdraw. Before she closed the door, I caught the glances that were once more exchanged between Portia and the serenely triumphant princess. I could see that Portia was maintaining her poise, meeting the beryl-green eyes of the Russian with an unyielding steadiness of gaze that disconcerted the princess, who after a moment withdrew her own angrily flashing orbs with sullen reluctance, the loser in that final duel between them.

As the limousine rolled away, Portia swung the bar that closed the gate, turned to me and clutched with one groping hand as if to keep herself from falling.

"It is the confirmation of my horrible suspicions," she said in a soft, broken voice. "Oh, Auntie, I am sick with the nausea that overwhelms me at this near approach of inconceivable evil!"

I put my arms about her comfortingly until she had regained her poise.

"Oh, poor Owen! Poor Owen!" she suddenly exclaimed in a voice betraying such keen anguish that I pushed her from me and held her at arm's length the better to see her face.

She met my eyes steadily with a confession of her love plain to see.

"Why 'poor Owen'?" I demanded.

"If I could only make you understand," she said, a desperate expression crossing her tortured face. "If I could only tell you all that I surmised, inferred, and must now accept against my own will," she ended, pitifully.

"Portia Delorme, the very best thing you can do now is to come into the house and eat your dinner. And after dinner you are going to try to tell me what you think I shall be able to understand, about this very mysterious situation. I'm referring," I said rather tartly, "to your strange and inexplicable and horribly rude behavior to that perfectly inoffensive woman. She must be gathering very pleasant conclusions about the good breeding of our American women," I finished sarcastically.

Portia bestowed a half-pitying, half-apologetic look upon me as she withdrew herself from my impatient grasp and preceded me into the dining room. It exasperated me, that look; it reminded me too strongly of the gaze with which a parent regards a child too young to grasp what the adult mind comprehends easily.

Portia's excitement did not keep her from eating a very good dinner, particularly as I represented to her that if she didn't eat she wouldn't have spunk enough to compete with her Russian rival. After dinner Fu served coffee in the library on a tabouret between Portia and myself, as we sat on piles of luxurious cushions.

My niece was deeply troubled at the incident of the flower, but whether it was for having permitted her temper to run away with her, or for having seen that signal sign of the princess' favor on her own cavalier, I wasn't sure. At last she put down her drained cup and leaned back among the pillows with a relaxed air. I waited, impatient for some explanation of her incomprehensible and—to me—ill-bred conduct.

"I suppose you think me a vulgarly jealous woman, Aunt Sophie. If you do, you do me an injustice. I admit that I was dizzy with nausea at the thought of that—that vile *thing*—in Owen's buttonhole, and especially at the bare idea that it had been placed there with intent by a—by the Princess Tchernova. Of course, you are mentally telling yourself that it could have been nothing but sheer jealousy on my part.

"Aunt Sophie, if you saw a loathsome and venomous insect upon my shoulder, wouldn't you strike at it, destroy it, without considering how your momentary blow would appear to onlookers? And if you knew that one of the onlookers had dropped the thing upon me for her—his—own wicked designs, would you hesitate because she—he—was watching?"

"My dear Portia, I'll admit that that—er—orchid, was about as unpleasant a bloom as I've ever seen, and had a most ungodly odor,"

I added viciously, "but you can't persuade me that it was a venomous thing designed by the princess to injure Owen. Why, any fool can see that she's deeply interested in. . ."

Portia interrupted impatiently. "That's just the point. She is interested. That's why I'm troubled. It isn't his body, it's his soul that I'm concerned about."

"But if she's interested, why should she wish to hurt him? Oh, Portia, don't you see how unjust your jealous suspicions are making you?"

I was heated. I couldn't help it. I didn't like the princess, but neither did I like my niece's incivility, if I may call it that, to a person who had done nothing to merit such pointed hostility, unless the flirtation with Owen might be called into evidence.

Portia shook both hands violently in front of her, with a gesture of hopelessness. Then she buried her face in both palms and I could see her shoulders shake gently. Portia was crying.

"My dear!" I was repentant for my harshness.

She lifted her face, all tear-stained, and regarded me with a kind of despair.

"That's just it, Aunt Sophie. I can't make you understand. It seems a paradox to you, doesn't it, when I say that the more Irma Tchemova cares for Owen, the greater is his danger? Oh, not from her love! Not from her love! But from what she may bring upon him, if he unhappily falls under her influence, as he is in a fair way of doing if she is unchecked in her designs."

"I'm afraid you will have to go a little further into detail, Portia," I managed to get out, wondering if her love and jealousy had unsettled her usually clear, unprejudiced judgment.

"Would you consider me mad, Aunt Portia, if I told you that the strange growth that creature put in poor Owen's buttonhole is capable of bringing down upon his head such terrible consequences that the mind can hardly conceive them?"

I tried to be judicial. If my niece's mind had become unbalanced, I must keep my own poise.

"I can believe that you believe, my dear, but I must confess that it seems impossible that there could be any sound basis for your belief."

"Other people besides me have not only believed such things, but have written them in some of these ancient—and modern—books." She waved her hand inclusively about the library walls, lined with volumes small and large, new, and mustily old. "Suppose I read selections from some of those books and try—try, Aunt Sophie!—To make things fairly clear to you. At least, from my own standpoint."

This sounded logical and eminently sensible. I told Portia so. She seemed relieved at my fair-mindedness, and my readiness to listen, at least. And so began one of the strangest, most brain-bewildering nights that I ever spent. All that night, until dawn broke, Portia read to me, talked to me, argued with me, explained to me, until—until I actually began to feel the faint glimmerings of probability in the mad and seemingly improbable propositions that she laid before me.

That such frightful monstrosities should exist seemed almost incredible, until Portia told me bluntly that I was like the old country man who, when confronted by a giraffe, stared incredulously, exclaiming "but they ain't no such animal!" My own personal ignorance of the existence of the strange anomaly called a *loup-garou* or werewolf was no proof that this traditional monster did not live. I was obliged to admit this, much to my own distaste. It is always hard to admit one's ignorance on any subject, especially to a younger person, someone of a newer generation.

That Portia had studied the subject under Mr. Differdale, I was prepared to admit; that he believed in lycanthropy, I could not deny; that he was a little bit "off," I assured myself secretly. Portia, however, kept dinning fact after fact at me, until I began to say, "seeing is believing," to which she replied with a rather pitying look, that she wouldn't wish upon her bitterest enemy an encounter with a werewolf, its brute-propensities intensified by the human intelligence that directed its actions.

The things upon which she based her suspicions were several. There was the coincidence of Sergei, the princess' chauffeur, having called his mistress "*volkodlak*" in his jealous passion, in my hearing. Portia read to me certain characteristics of the fabled werewolves, and pointed out their similarity to certain of the princess' striking and individual peculiarities. "The werewolf," ran one account, "cannot eat sugar, but turns from it with loathing. Nor can it drink any sweet cordials. Raw flesh in any form is its principal food, and a fresh kill is the favorite meat meal." There were here the coincidences of the princess' refusing sugar and sweets at the Differdale-Arnold home the afternoon that I had tea with them, and the plentiful supply of raw meat Gus Stieger had been ordered to send daily to the princess' residence—for her wolves!

As for more intimate personal characteristics, there were the beryl-green eyes that in dusk gleamed like garnets; the sharp white teeth; the small, low-set ears, pointed above (I had seen one escaping from the closely bound hair when the princess removed her ermine cap); the over-red lips; the narrowed lids under eyebrows that curved down to meet at the foot of the nose. There were the oval, tinted, highly-polished nails on the slender fingers, with the third finger so abnormally long. Even the princess' slinking, sinuous walk, Portia pointed out, by its resemblance to the tireless gait of a wolf, would have betrayed her real personality to an expert. But I suppose I'm getting too far ahead. I must set down here, for the benefit of those who are not familiar with the subject, what Portia's conclusions were in regard to that evil personality.

II

From what Portia said, it appears that from time immemorial there have been people whose faith in the Evil One or his angels has been so complete that it has enabled them to work miracles of evil, just as faith in good enables others to work miracles of good. It is the faith that does the work, just as the same electricity can light our houses or kill us, according to how it is handled and directed.

These infatuated people who believe in the Evil One are actually metamorphosed—either at their own desire for some personal reason, or by someone evilly disposed toward them—into the form of a wolf, so that at nighttime they are impelled to go about mauling, killing and eating small animals, such as rabbits or sheep, until they come to the point where they prey upon human beings.

At just this point, I can divide my readers into two distinct factions. There are those who are saying: "Oh, this is a wild tale! But then, it makes fair reading to pass an idle hour." There are those others who are devouring my every word with tight lips and fixed eyes; *those others who know.*

For the benefit of my two classes of readers I shall say that I do not intend to attempt the proof of my sanity or the disproof of my credulity; I leave that momentous judgment to them. For the personal opinion of the class that believes all this a fanciful tale, I don't care; I am writing, from now on, for those few who know that I am penning a tragic and incredible truth. But I shall sketch a few logical points that may help my incredulous first class readers to understand the story; at least they shall not complain that I am asking them to swallow the impossible, without an apparently sound fictional basis upon which to build.

That there are entities good and evil existing in the ether "in which we live, and move, and have our being," is today indisputable; only a very ignorant person dares now deny the existence of what he has not happened to realize in his own limited personal experience. These entities may even be drawn into material form; solid, living, breathing flesh, to all appearance. I need go into no details; one way of doing this is through the services of a good medium, and the other by ancient spells, known to the initiated. Certain of these entities are men and women who have "died" and left their bodies of flesh on this earth-plane; others are entities which have never been housed in flesh and blood but have always existed on the astral plane of life.

Some of these latter entities possess the power of granting requests made by those who call upon them, provided always that the suppliant worshiper has sufficient faith in that power. It may not please religious bigots to have me point out that in the Bible the great Teacher stated definitely that His followers would in time be able to do greater works than He, provided that they would follow certain procedures, which He explained to them exhaustively. He cursed the fig-tree to show His disciples that the Universal Power could be as easily drawn upon for unjust, as for good, purposes. He even drew their attention to the blighted tree with a careful warning to be very particular about forgiving their enemies before attempting to use this Universal Power, as a precaution against their misuse, in anger, of an impersonal power that is at the initiate's disposal for evil as well as for good.

There are certain of these evil entities which can confer upon a believer the privilege of metamorphosing—or appearing to do so, which seems to me to be about the same—into the shape of a savage wild beast, usually a wolf. This tradition exists in every European country, even in Asia, in one form or another. Germany, France, Russia, all the Balkan countries, abound with tales of werewolves. Irish legends tell how St. Patrick turned Vereticus, King of Wales, into a wolf; of how St. Natalis cursed an illustrious Irish family so effectually that each member of it was doomed to be a wolf for seven years. In Iceland the *berserkir* averred their ability to metamorphose into bears and wolves, and they dressed themselves in skins of these animals in support of their pretensions. In England, as late as these modern days, a young woman artist, returning from a painting expedition through a wild and lonely countryside, had a most alarming and unpleasant experience with what can only be called the fantasm of a werewolf. The incident—and there are others, also—is sufficiently well authenticated to go on record as a fact. Let me remind the too-cynical reader that today no one can deny the existence of what were once generally called scoffingly "ghosts," and a thing can hardly have a ghost without once having existed in the flesh.

Scientists have proved that everything in the universe is composed of infinitesimal intelligences which I believe they call electrons. These tiny entities have what certain religious denominations term "free will"; they are able to repel or attract other electrons as they choose. It is conceivable that if each electron has intelligence and will of its own, it can, to a certain extent, select its companionship, shape its environment. When electrons are grouped together in a certain manner, such as in a human body, there is always a central, or group will, that governs them in certain functions for the benefit of the group. The group will, for example, commands all voluntary movements consciously and can learn by practise how to command the so-called involuntary functions of the body-group; this has been proved by scientific experiment.

The thing that starts the group will to functioning is an abstract thing; a thought; an idea. A thought held in a man's mind or imagination can make him ill. Conversely, it can make him well if he is sick. It is strange that humanity prefers to accept but half of this proposition. Mankind readily believes that unhappy thoughts will depress it, but mankind has not yet learned to think, consciously, the happy thoughts that will uplift it. The electrons of the body-group are just as ready and willing to aceept, and act upon, agreeable thoughts as upon disagreeable thoughts.

THE BIBLE, AS A BOOK of practical science, leaves nothing more to be asked for. It puts natural science plainly before the eyes of the reader that he usually considers it too easy, hence too good to believe, so he tells himself that the promises weren't meant to function in modem days, only in ancient times! Yet we are told over and over in the Bible that the individual will at the head of each body-group, the will that we call our Ego, can do anything it pleases; no limits are imposed, *provided only that it will follow the natural laws for producing certain results*. The great Teacher expounded the Law in Faith:

"Whosoever does not doubt in his heart, but believeth that what he saith shall come to pass, he shall have whatsoever he saith." These words in themselves are sufficient for a practical, working philosophy of life. Moreover, in performing his so-called miracles, he told sick people: "According to *your* faith be it unto you." The Bible tells us that in his hometown, where he was well known, Jesus was *unable* to perform "miracles." Why? Because die people there couldn't raise themselves to any very high state of faith in the carpenter's son whom they had known as a boy.

I am not trying to instruct anybody in religious faith, but trying to show that the Bible teaches that nothing is impossible of performance that is asked in absolute faith. If, instead of a firm and steadfast faith in God's power to do all things, we substitute as firm a faith in an evil entity's ability to work unlimited evil, are we not turning Universal Power into materialization through the same channel of faith, merely altering conditions of transmission? In other words, when God-power flows through the medium of man's imagination, it must by its own law perform what it is called upon to do through unwavering faith, whether that deed be intended by the group will of that man's body as good or evil. Electricity is differentiated in power and results by man's intervention; Godpower is subject to natural laws just as is electricity.

The carpenter's son proved his mission by his works. When He, therefore, tells me that I can have anything, or do anything, provided only that I *believe without doubting* that such things can be had or done, where is the inspired idiot who will dare rise up to tell me that God has limitations, "especially in modern times," and not hide a shamed head for his own inconsistency in professing belief in promises that he declares aren't workable. . . "except spiritually," this last being a sop to his own incredulity. The god is clay who cannot make good his promises, and the God I worship isn't made of clay. His promises hold good today just as they held good thousands of years ago, because they are based on natural law.

I see no more reason, then, to discredit the statements of some individuals that by exercising their faith in certain directions they can metamorphose into wolf-form, than I see reason to discredit the statements scattered all through the Bible which make complete faith the only desideratum to obtaining all things. Aren't good and evil opposite poles of the same magnet?

All this, and more, my niece Portia pointed out to me in our all-night session. I may frankly admit that although I was a skeptic before we began that memorable conversation, I emerged from it with a new and astonishing viewpoint on the phenomena of life.

III

My niece kept on talking and arguing until daylight surprised us at our gruesome subject, and until she was assured that she had at least brought me to that open frame of mind when all I wanted was proof, more proof, of what to her was as clear as the daylight filtering through the silken curtains.

"But if the Princess Tchemova is a werewolf," I said, distastefully, the new word with its bizarre conception coming reluctantly from my tongue, which hated to voice so seemingly absurd a thing, "what do you intend to do about it?"

"With your assistance, Aunt Sophie, I intend to save Owen from her wicked designs. I—I will go to any length, to prevent her making him what I believe her to be already. I would even attempt a projection of my astral body—and that is a dangerous, a very dangerous thing."

I was inexpressibly shocked and alarmed. It is one thing to become such a monstrosity voluntarily; quite another to have the metamorphosis forced upon one. Portia replied to my horrified look with a stern expression.

"Perhaps you begin to understand now that I was not experiencing vulgar jealousy when I stripped that loathsome lycanthropic bit of rank growth from Owen's lapel?"

"Do you mean, Portia Delorme, that the Princess Tehernova is trying to make a werewolf out of Owen Edwardes?"

"That is exactly what I mean. Aunt Sophie. My action in destroying it was prompted by the love of one soul for the salvation of another soul," she said, slowly and thoughtfully. "But—he is safe only for the moment. Didn't she say that she had 'many others'? Oh, I read her meaning, just as she meant I should! She did not refer to that horrid growth alone, but to other—other means of accomplishing her fell purpose."

"Then she doesn't really want to make a meal out of Owen?" I ventured, uncomfortably aware that I was tacitly accepting my niece's amazing conclusions.

"No!" passionately. "It would be better, far better, if it were only this ordinary danger to which he is exposed. What threatens Owen is a far more subtle, far more terrible thing. Irma Tchemova intends, because of her infatuation for him, to transform him by her arts, her knowledge of the means to do so, into a companion werewolf for herself. It is not his body that is so much in danger; it is his soul that stands in such deadly peril that the very thought of it sickens me."

"Why don't you warn him?"

"About how much would he listen to, without thinking that I had taken leave of my senses!" demanded my niece, helplessly. "No, I cannot tell him anything. I can only try to attach him to me so deeply that he will avoid that creature's propinquity."

She colored.

"If I were you, Portia Delorme, and I believed the man I loved was in such deadly peril, I'd go to see him the very first thing tomorrow—that is, this morning—and let him know that I accepted his attentions definitely. After that, he won't feel like letting another woman stick flowers in his coat lapel. That is, if you'll see to it that your flowers go there first."

"I believe you're right, Aunt Sophie." Portia sprang up from her cushions with surprising spirit, when you consider that we'd been talking all night. "I'm going to get dressed this minute—"

"Do have breakfast first," I urged, somewhat alarmed at my niece's abrupt decision. (I myself like to turn a thing over in my mind carefully before acting).

Portia laughed and ran out of the room. She came back in an astonishingly short time, attired for the street. Her face shone with the happiness of hope; her eyes sparkled vividly. She hesitated a moment beside me (by this time I was having breakfast, preparatory to taking a good long nap to make up for my wakeful night), suddenly bent, and kissed me warmly.

It did not seem fifteen minutes before she returned, wearing an entirely different air. Her face was grim; her lips met in a tight line of determination. Her eyes glowed darkly. She dropped into a chair opposite me (I had not yet finished my cup of Fu Sing's excellent coffee) and stared unseeingly across the room as if in a trance.

"Portia! Did you see him!"

I was as excited as a girl over her first sweetheart.

"Yes, Aunt Sophie. I saw him—and—her."

"What? At this early hour—?"

"Do the powers of evil limit themselves to the hours of darkness?" she parried, looking up and meeting my eyes with that same look of stern determination on her face that I had noticed when she entered the room.

"She was there on some excuse about the papers for the transfer of the Burnham house. I—I had to wait in the outer office, while she"—with bitter accent—"wound him more hopelessly within her toils. I presume you'd like to know what I overheard? I assure you that I personally have no scruples at listening to anything and everything that the Princess Tchernova may say.

"'Is it possible that the odor of the marigold is disagreeable to your nostrils?' the princess was questioning Owen, as if in wonder, as Portia came into the outer office. 'But there—how stupid of me! I remember that when I was a little, little girl, I rather disliked it myself. I remember, yes, my Ow-een, that I did not care for the perfume of the marigold. Until—well, I grew to love it, for it was a flower very dear to my father, who grew many marigold flowers on his estate. Now you can understand, of course, that Irma loves the marigold because it reminds her of the happy days she will never know again.'"

She sighed softly.

Owen must have reproached himself inwardly for his lack of tact, for through the glass partition Portia saw him put out his hand impulsively to take the yellow flower from the slender hand of the Russian. He put it into his lapel himself. Irma smiled at him with a pretty gratefulness. Although she must have seen Portia approach and enter the office, she feigned to know nothing of her rival's nearness.

"'Some day you shall see my so-wonderful orchids,' exclaimed she, as if this were an afterthought. 'You will be interested in my orchids; they are so weird, so bizarre—'

"'I'm afraid I don't deserve your kindness, princess. I'm rather a matter-of-fact chap, you see, and a simple field flower means more to me than these freaks you mention. However,' hastily, 'I'll come, of course, to see your orchids if you wish me to do so.'

"'They have been brought from all over the world, Ow-een. Some from Germany, some from France, some from India, and oh, the wonderful orchids from my Russia! They are well worth coming to see, my Ow-een. And—soon you will love them as Irma loves them—wear them always as Irma wears them. Ah, I know, my Ow-een; they are irresistible.'

She pronounced her English with a delicate precision that sounded charmingly on unprejudiced ears. She knew very well the powerful charm of a language spoken with a slight accent and funny little irregularities; it makes a man feel that the pretty speaker is an ingenuous infant, not a grown woman capable of using every feminine weapon with deadly intent and purpose. Portia could not stand the strain any longer, and the knowledge that the other woman knew beyond doubt that she was waiting without was too much for her already strained nerves. She stepped to the inner office door and spoke to Owen in a casually friendly manner, inviting him to have dinner with us that same evening.

"'So sorry, Portia,' Owen said, going toward her disturbedly; 'but I've just promised the princess to spend the evening with her. There are so many things about the Bumham house that need attention,' he hastened to explain, at the look that must have come into Portia's eyes.

"'Again, have I made the Intrusion?' cried the princess vivaciously, her tongue caressing her red lips rapidly as if tasting something particularly palatable.

Portia, who surmised that it was her own possible discomfiture that so pleased the other woman, hastened to reply indifferently that Mr. Edwardes might care to drop in some evening in the near future, when he didn't happen to be engaged. She managed to make the invitation so casual that the Russian, she said afterward to me, actually looked disappointed.

"Then Owen's going to dine with that creature tonight?"

"Yes, Auntie," she admitted, her brow drawn thoughtfully.

"What—what are we going to do to save Owen?"

At the tremor that I could not keep out of my voice, my niece suddenly gave me a searching look, leaned her head on her hands on the table, and burst into wrenching sobs, greatly to my alarm and mystification.

"Don't mind. I'll be all right in another few minutes," she managed to tell me between sobs. "I'm crying, dear, because I think you're beginning to see the terrible gravity of the situation; because I think you're beginning to realize that Hamlet's words to Horatio were only too true."

She dried her eyes at length, and regained her self-control.

"Owen will be there in that woman's house tonight, Aunt Sophie, subject to Heaven only knows what devilish machinations on her part. About Sergei, her chauffeur, I am not yet quite certain; I have never seen him near by when he was not muffled in furs, and—oh, his very fondness for those enveloping furs may point to his—. You see, Aunt Sophie, how bewildered the brain becomes that attempts to cope with tins terrible subject?"

"Is there anything we can do to prevent her harming Owen?" I demanded nervously. I was in the strange mental condition when I believed and disbelieved at the same time, see-sawing back and forth as Portia talked and I reflected.

"No. Yes!" cried my niece. "We can watch and see what she does. Perhaps in this way I may learn something, or prevent something. Forewarned is forearmed, Aunt Sophie, and all's fair in love and war," she finished enigmatically. "Would you go with me again, on such questionable business as this of peering into other people's windows."

"Portia Delorme, if you intend to stick your head into the lion's mouth—I mean, the wolf's mouth—do you think I'm going to desert you? And didn't I go poking into her window with you once before?"

I was indignant at her questioning me. She jumped up then and went to the door, turning before she went down the hall.

"I'm going into the library, to read up some more on lycanthropy. And then I'll probably be busy in my laboratory for quite sometime. Don't expect to see me until dinnertime. If you'll manage to be ready by then, we can be out of the house as soon as it's dark."

I tried to curb my excitement, but found this a difficult matter. After dark we two women were going out to spy upon the Princess Tchernova. And we were justifying our action by telling ourselves that this lovely Russian woman was a fiend in human form, a demon from whose wicked schemes Owen Edwardes had much to fear! Why, the thing was so bizarre that it made me laugh aloud with incredulity one minute, and stop my own laughter with horrified shrinking and backward glances the next.

How I got through that day, I don't know. The approaching excitement buoyed me up, of course, but I remember that I entirely lost my appetite for lunch, and could hardly taste the delicious dinner that Fu had prepared with his usual painstaking care. I put on the same clothes I had worn on the night when Portia and I had first looked into the princess' windows, in order to be as inconspicuous as possible. At dinner I noted that Portia was wearing breeches and a heavy dark coat short enough not to impede walking—or running.

While Portia ate her dinner in silence, with only a casual nod across the table to me, I thought over the preposterous things she had read and told me the night before, and recalled the marvelous powers she had claimed for Mr. Differdale, powers which I secretly began to hope my niece shared, considering the errand we were contemplating.

IV

We went out of the house before dusk and made a considerable detour by dark, to avoid observation or comment by people of the neighborhood. We had left the dogs at home. Portia did not even mention taking them, although they followed us wistfully to the gate, and whined plaintively when it closed after us. I presume she did not wish to risk alarming the inmates of the Burnham

We entered the grounds from the farther side, opposite Queens Boulevard, and crept silently toward the house, guided by lights that flashed from the tall windows of the lower floor. We had but a momentary glimpse into the dining hall; just as we came within good seeing distance, Sergei appeared at the window and pulled together the long dark draperies of heavy brocaded silk.

I was so disappointed that I let out an exclamation which chagrined me terribly for fear Portia had overheard my indiscretion, but she appeared not to have heard me, so preoccupied was she with the problem before us. I have always envied men for their freedom of expression: the relief they seem to find in a curse-word always appears enormous. It is indicative of the high tension under which I labored, that when Sergei pulled the curtains together, robbing Portia and me of what we had come especially to see, I emitted a single short and savage word. I said, with fervor: "Damn!" I cannot really be sorry, even today, that I said it; I felt afterward—apart from my fear that Portia had overheard it—as if that expletive had been a safety-valve to my feelings.

While I stewed over the possibility of Portia's having heard me disgrace myself, my niece was busily engaged in peeping and peering from the ground to see if there were not some tiny openings in the hangings, and apparently she did find one, for she remained with her face glued to the cold pane. When I saw this, I went at once to the window nearest her and found that I was as fortunate as she, for the heavy curtains had been dragged against high-piled rugs, resulting in V-Shaped openings at the bottom, just where our eyes came as we stood outside on the terrace that ran about the house. What we saw was innocent enough, so much so that I began to blame Portia in my mind for having brought me on a most undignified wild goose chase.

The whole room was magnificent to the extreme, but it was of that type of splendor that reeks of barbarism with its display of vivid colors, flashing semi-precious stones, gorgeous draperies and pictured hangings and embroideries. It was not at all the land of room you would have expected from the exterior of the old Burnham house with its very dignified architecture and generally sober aspect. My eyes ached after a minute's trying to distinguish objects through that small opening, particularly as the room was illuminated by several dozen candles, the light of which was broken up into hundreds of dancing, blinding facets of dazzling brilliance by the dangling cut-glass ornaments that festooned each candlestick.

A table occupied the center of the room, a table that stood about a foot higher than the rich velvet rugs covering the floor. What seemed a richly embroidered, lace-encrusted white linen cover was spread upon it, and silver, glass and china glittered and sparkled and gleamed above it. Around the table great masses of richly colored cushions were piled. Reclining among them, her back to the window, was the Princess Tchernova. She was wearing a daring costume, cut down to her waistline in back, and nothing but straps of diamonds held it at the shoulders. Her arms sparkled with many-colored gems.

Owen Edwardes occupied a pile of cushions opposite his hostess, but unless I am a mighty poor judge of human nature he was extremely ill at ease. He leaned among the pillows as if he did not enjoy them very much, and evidently found it awkward to eat in that half-reclining position.

The room was full of great vases overflowing with yellow marigold blooms. Where the princess could have procured them at that time of the year I don't know, unless she had standing orders for her favorite flowers with florists in a position to supply her. The stench of those unsavory-smelling blooms must have permeated every crack and crevice of the room; I actually imagined that I smelled it from where I stood outside the closed window, so many of those glowing flowers were there. The princess wore a huge corsage bouquet of marigolds and I noticed a yellow dot of color resting on the lapel of Owen's unpretentious business suit.

Sergei was serving his mistress and her guest, entering from the swinging door that led to the butler's pantry whenever the princess clapped her hands, Oriental fashion. As I stared, my head on one side so that both eyes could look through the opening simultaneously, Irma clapped both palms, leaning across to her companion and smiling as she chatted vivaciously. Sergei brought in a crystal tray and set it down upon the table before his mistress. On it stood a tall, curiously cut decanter of some clear liquor that sparkled as if with an inner life of its own. Two slender goblets of gold stood beside the decanter.

Irma waved the retainer from the room. Still talking to Owen, her narrow eyes regarding him provocatively from under lowered lids, she leaned forward and began pouring that bubbling, springing, living liquid into one of the golden goblets. As she poured, I was unutterably startled to hear a gasp come out of the darkness near me, from where my niece Portia stood staring through the adjoining window.

"Not that, dear God! *Not that*!" she half groaned, half prayed. And then all at once I felt my hand grasped and a strong tug drew me away from the house and in the direction of the boulevard.

I screamed. I couldn't have helped it to save my life. For the moment I was so taken by surprise that I was unnerved completely. All the horrible things that had been recounted to me during the vigil of the preceding night seemed to have come crashing about me.

"Scream!" That was Portia's injunction, as she ran beside me and pulled me along with her in the direction of the lighted stores that line the opposite side of the boulevard. "Scream! Keep it up! Your scream is much shriller than mine, Aunt Sophie."

She was aiming, I soon saw, at reaching the protection of the lighted street and the police-signal shelter, but all at once she stopped short and drew me down behind the sheltering concealment of a winter shrub. The pounding feet of running men came down the walk toward us, and as they whirled by in the darkness I thought I recognized the heavy body of Sergei and in front of him the athletic form of Owen.

The curtains on this, the other side of the house, were now being drawn apart, and before one window, her lithe form outlined darkly against the brilliant lights within, stood the princess, staring out into the garden. Although common sense told me that she could not have seen our crouching figures against that fir-tree, my heart began to beat quickly with sick apprehension. Still Portia held me down firmly, until the sound of a police-whistle shrilled to our ears across the dark grounds, and the voices of men calling excitedly rose from the boulevard. We could see dark figures emerging from lighted stores. Then Portia pulled at my hand and whispered guardedly:

"Don't expose yourself, Aunt Sophie, anymore than you can help. But we can't go out by the boulevard now, with the police on the lookout, and we've got to risk crossing the grounds again to the other side, and going down the Burnham Road to the subway station. We'll be safer inside the station than out here in the open. I wish I'd brought Andrei and Boris," she finished regretfully.

THE EXCITEMENT ON THE BOULEVARD continued to grow, but was apparently centered about the police shelter. Portia and I crept warily from behind our shelter, like two criminals. I noticed that she had taken off her coat and was running in flannel shirt and knickers, and it erossed my mind that she had done it on purpose, for in the uncertain light she would readily have passed as a man. We heard no pursuing footsteps, but as we gained the other side of the house grounds, I could hear the snarling of the wolves in their den at the foot of the garden; disturbed, probably, by the unusual sounds. I certainly hoped the cement and steel cage would prove as strong as it had looked when Owen showed

By the time we had gotten a couple of blocks away and could see our goal looming darkly ahead of us across the fields on the other side of the subway line, we had regained our confidence, if not our breath. I observed to Portia then, that I never had thought that I could run as I had that night.

"You ran like an old dear, if not a young deer," she punned mischievously. "Oh, Aunt Sophie, I would never have forgiven myself if they'd caught you peering into the princess' windows."

I couldn't help laughing. "How about you, my dear?"

"It wouldn't have mattered about me," she said quickly. "I can take care of myself. I'm prepared for all emergencies. But you—your faith, dear Auntie, is the blind faith that isn't very reliable because it isn't founded on knowledge of irrefutable logical truths. Mine—mine is the cultivated faith that believes because it knows—because it has demonstrated those truths."

"Then you're not talking about Owen, and the storekeepers, my dear?" I said, rather puzzled.

"Oh, no! It was—wolves—I was troubled about. If I'd given you a sprig of this ash and told you the formula to repeat in case of an attack by a werewolf, do you suppose you would have had the faith to believe that it wasn't all mummery?"

I couldn't reply, so I remained silent.

"You see?" sadly.

I most certainly wouldn't have expected to rout a ravenous supernatural beast with a sprig of an ash tree and an abracadabra exorcism. Portia was quite right. If she knew, or believed that she knew, that the ashsprig would be efficacious under such circumstances, then she was protected; if not by the ash, by her belief in it.

We walked briskly along, stopping occasionally while Portia listened. The excitement about the boulevard and the Burnham place had died down, but it seemed to me that I could hear the pattering feet of something behind us, something like a big dog. I communicated my alarm to my niece by grasping at her hand and pointing wordlessly in the direction of the sound. She turned her head and appeared to be trying to pierce the darkness. Then she pushed upon me a rough sprig of something that she broke from a spray which I now noticed she was wearing at her girdle.

"Take this, and if you can possibly believe in it, believe! Pray, Aunt Portia, pray!" she whispered tensely. "Something is following us. I don't know if it is some big dog, or if the princess has let out one of her pets— or if she herself. . ." and then her surmises died away into silence as she took my hand in hers and urged me into a run again.

By this time we had come to the corner of Burnham Road and Gilman Street. As we reached that corner, Portia jerked me around it and pulled me into the comparative shelter of the overhanging wall. She pressed the button, at the same time applying her key to the lock, without waiting for Fu to open the door from within. She pushed the bronze door open and pushed me into the aperture, backing in after me.

Just as we shrank into that niche in the wall, there came the sound of something scratching on the pavement at the corner, and then a dark, heavy body hurtled through the air and past the opening with a savage snarl that sent my blood cold. Hardly had Portia closed the door (it closed with a spring lock), than the heavy thudding feet of that unknown beast that had dogged our footsteps came scratching against the metal.

Boris and Andrei had been let out into the enclosure by Fu, and came springing and bounding to us, only to stop as if petrified at the sound of that scratching. Portia stood between them motionless, absolutely silent, her attitude that of the utmost concentration, her head thrown proudly up as if in secret defiance of that which was without. After a long minute, there came an ugly, quavering howl that made me clutch at her in apprehension.

"Portia! It can't get in, can it?" I whispered tensely.

She shook an impatient head and returned to her concentration. The sound of those padding feet went softly from the doorway and melted into the quiet of the spring night.

Now that the danger was past, I permitted myself the luxury of nerves.

"Why didn't it attack us while we were walking across the fields?" I inquired, almost hysterically, checking a tendency to laugh and cry at once.

"I think she was afraid," said Portia.

"Oh, my dear, you don't mean that you think it was. . . *she*?"

"What do you suppose it was? It was she herself, or it was one of her wolves."

"Is there anything we can do now—I mean, about Owen?"

"No, Auntie. Owen won't go back tonight, to drink that—that poison with her. He will be told that she is indisposed; that the excitement has been too much for her. No, he will not find—her. Now do try to get a few winks of sleep, Auntie; I feel the need of rest myself."

We went quietly into the house. Boris stuck to me, for which I felt very thankful; I disliked the idea of going to bed in a room that would have seemed peopled with phantom beasts that leered upon me with beryl-green eyes, and Boris meant company.

As Portia was about to leave me in the corridor, I asked her something that had roused my curiosity.

"What was it that the princess was pouring out for Owen into those golden goblets, Portia? You called it poison just now, and I wonder. . ."

"Poison? Well, so it is. Didn't you notice how alive that clear liquid seemed, with its bubble and sparkle and constant motion, even when the bottle still stood on the tray? That water has undoubtedly been brought by the Princess Tchemova from Russia, from some lycanthropous stream."

"Then. . . ?"

"It impregnates the person who drinks it with the curse of lycanthropy."

I was sick with horror. I leaned back against the doorframe and stared at Portia.

"Do you suppose we were in time?"

"If you hadn't screamed when I touched you, I was going to scream myself. Your shriek was timed as if you had rehearsed it beforehand. It served my purpose. Owen heard it, and must have sprung away from the table before that evil beverage had moistened his lips. It was only a moment before he was out in the grounds, hunting for the woman who had screamed out of the night." She laughed, but without real mirth. "If you hadn't precipitated matters by your scream, I would either have screamed, or have taken the risk of breaking in upon them and begging Owen not to drink, for my sake, no matter what he thought of me."

"I'm afraid I shall be nervous tonight, Portia," I told her, rather quaveringly. "Do you suppose it—she—could get into this house!"

"This house is safe from such invasions, for the present, dear. You can sleep soundly. But if you are wakeful tonight, call me. I shall hear you, even if you whisper, for my whole being is on the watch."

She kissed me, and I went into my own room. I must admit that I did not get into a sound sleep before morning, for I was haunted by memories of those padding footsteps that had come up behind us in the dark. I began to understand what it meant to feel real fear, and told myself that I would not venture out after dark either with or without Boris.

V

Part II

WHEN I WENT DOWN TO the stores the next morning, it was to find everybody in a great state of excitement. Gus Stieger, weighing the steak I had ordered, told me about it with gusto.

It appears that about dark a woman had been heard screaming "Help! Help!" from the grounds of the Burnham house, and that Owen Edwardes, who had been dining with the Princess Tehemova, rushed out with the chauffeur and searched everywhere but without result. Then the two men rushed down to the police station, and the officer sounded his whistle for other assistance, and disappeared into the darkness to search the grounds himself. Those of the storekeepers who were keeping open a bit later, among them Gus, saw O'Brien's flashlight occasionally as he went here and there on the grounds. They waited for him to come back until nearly midnight, then closed up their stores.

"And believe me. Miss Delorme, he ain't showed up yet!"

My heart nearly skipped a beat. Had the genial O'Brien fallen a victim to it—to her? I felt as if I could not wait to get back to Portia with this terrible and unexpected news, although what she could do I didn't know.

"They've got a new man at the station," chimed in the yoiee of a woman, and I turned to meet the eyes of Mrs. Differdale, wearing a new boudoir cap of pink satin and white lace, in which she felt quite coquettish and dressed up. "A new man named Murphy. You see, Miss Delorme, they've found poor O'Brien's electric torch lying just outside the wolfden, and they're thinking one of the wolves ate him or something. They say there's one brute missing."

"That's rather silly," I murmured, trying to gather my scattered wits. In another moment, thought I, she'd be blaming Boris or Andrei, and I must be ready for her.

"Were Portia's wolfhounds out last night?" bluntly inquired she.

I realized that she had only been waiting to ask me that question.

"Why?" I queried innocently.

Her eyes avoided mine self-consciously.

"Oh, I don't know," she said vaguely.

But she did know, and she knew that I knew, that she was trying her best to accuse those noble dogs of killing and then devouring O'Brien.

I couldn't help smiling ironically as I remarked that both dogs had been in my room with me all that evening. She wasn't half-pleased with my assurance, I could see, but couldn't very well continue with her half-veiled insinuations, after my direct statement.

On the way home I ran into Owen Edwardes, coming out of the hardware store.

"I'll drive you home, Aunt Sophie," he commanded, rather than asked.

I surmised that he wanted to say something about the previous night, and I was not wrong.

"It's an odd thing, Aunt Sophie, that I felt Portia so vividly in my mind last night that I could have sworn she was within a few feet of me." (I concealed an ill-timed smile). "When that woman screamed, I had the terrible premonition that it was Portia who was in deadly peril. Of course, common sense told me that she was home shut safely behind the Differdale walls," dryly.

"Well?" I encouraged.

"There wasn't a sign of anything anywhere, although the Princess Tchemova's man hunted with me over every inch of the grounds, and as soon as O'Brien joined us we had his electric torch. By the way, it is a very strange thing that O'Brien should have disappeared off the face of the earth. What do you suppose could have become of him?"

What did I suppose! I felt my brain whirling with sick surmises: a faint feeling seized upon me, but I tried to reply as collectedly as possible.

"He'll probably turn up sometime today," I ventured.

"I have a feeling that he won't," Owen said in stubborn contradiction. "Just why I should feel so positive I don't know, but I do. Funny, isn't it? No, I don't think any of us will see O'Brien again. I'm afraid something has happened to him. What, I can't guess—but something."

I could not speak, then; Owen's words were too close to what I suspected, what I dreaded, from Portia's disclosures to me. I could not meet Owen's frank, inquiring eyes.

"I wish you'd tell Portia," he went on after a moment's pause, "that the princess is considering altering various things about the Burnham house and insists upon asking my opinion on every change. I suppose that when they are finished, I won't be making so many visits, Aunt Sophie. Just now," he finished, rather vaguely, "I really—well—you understand—I can't exactly—help myself."

I understood far better than he thought I did. I began to think I knew why he couldn't—exactly—help himself, poor Owen! What he wanted was reassurance from me as to Portia's complete understanding of the situation. How little he realized that my niece knew more than he could possibly have suspected!

"I'm sure Portia understands," I managed to tell him. "If she doesn't, I do, Owen."

At that use of his first name, he turned and looked me full in the eyes with such a grateful smile that it warmed my heart.

"That sounds good to me, Aunt Sophie," he said softly, with a bit of emphasis upon my name, in turn.

We drew up before the Differdale gateway.

"I don't suppose Portia cares to go to the theater with me some evening next week?" he ventured wistfully.

"It's time—don't you think?—That she began to go out a little, for her own sake."

I may have been unwise, but I couldn't help speaking a bit sharply. "It's high time, Owen, that she began to cultivate the acquaintance of people of her own age," I snapped.

"It's too bad she doesn't seem to care for the princess, isn't it? The princess seems to have taken a strong liking to her, and often wonders why Portia hasn't called on her. Really, my fair client isn't so dreadful, when one gets to know her. She always treats me royally; insists upon making me eat and drink all kinds of native Russian dishes everytime I go to her house. And you ought to see her orchids! They are certainly gorgeous plants, although I must admit I don't care a whole lot for them myself. They have such a sickly, faintish odor, all of them, in spite of their vivid, fascinating colors. And I never did care for flowers with thick fleshy petals and sticky soap oozing out of their stems; I prefer the honest field flowers, or perhaps a more ethereal type of orchid. After all, it's just a matter of taste, I presume."

I rang the bell and Owen drove away after he had watched me enter the gateway. I think he would have liked to pursue further the question of Portia's attending the theater with him, but didn't exactly dare say much more than he had already said.

PORTIA WAS BREAKFASTING WHEN I went into the dining room to look for her, after finding she was not in her own room. She put down her coffee cup and lifted her eyes intently to my face, studying it.

"What has happened now?"

"O'Brien has been missing since last night. The only trace they've found of the man is his electric torch near the wolfden of the old Burnham house. And they say that one of the wolves is missing; that it must have gotten out and made away with O'Brien."

My niece drew a long breath, her eyes deeply troubled.

"I'm sorry. I'm very sorry. But I'm helpless to avert these—disappearances. I can do nothing until it is too late. That is the awful thing about it. If the princess should take a fancy to some child in the neighborhood, and I were to warn its mother, do you think my words would be taken seriously? The mother would believe me insane, of course. That's why I can't help things."

Her words touched a faint memory. It stirred formlessly as I listened to her lamentation, then suddenly took shape.

"Portia! Minna Arnold!"

My tones must have been horror-stricken as I sank into a chair opposite my niece, for her face was a shade paler as she leaned across the table toward me.

"What about Minna?" Her tone was sharp and her expression much disturbed; her clear eyes were wide as she watched me.

"Portia, I can't seem to collect my thoughts properly. It's too frightful to suspect any human being of such—such calculation, such wicked scheming." I gulped.

"Try to calm yourself, Auntie, for heaven's sake! There's too much at stake. I grant the child isn't very appealing, but if danger threatens Mr. Differdale's little niece, I must run the risk of being considered insane, and warn Aurora Arnold."

"You know I went to your sister-in-law's the other day for a cup of tea, Portia? The princess was there. She made a good deal of Minna. I can remember distinctly that she was disturbed because Alice was so thin, and it turned out that she had been giving Minna large boxes of expensive chocolates. Minna has been going to her house to get them, two or three times a week. Mrs. Arnold said that the child had been eating too many sweets, and the princess declared that the next box should be for Alice, so that she would grow plump like her sister."

Portia laid her napkin on the table and got slowly to her feet. She did not look very happy over the prospect of what she probably felt it her duty.

"I'll have to go over at once, Auntie. Alice is in deadly danger. Minna, too; perhaps more than Alice."

"But what will you tell Mrs. Arnold, Portia?"

My niece looked past me with eyes that seemed to see beyond the open doorway. She sighed deeply.

"Auntie, I don't know. I'll have to trust to the Powers of Light"—she often referred to what she called "beneficent entities" as "Powers of Light"—"to put the right words into my mouth when I am there. I'd better go and dress now. I'll take the dogs. The poor beasts haven't been outside for twenty-four hours; a long run will do them good."

As Portia told me afterward, she found Aurora Arnold at home, but the older woman had not returned from her marketing—or gossiping. Aurora pretended to be afraid of Andrei and Boris.

"I wish you wouldn't bring them here, Portia," she said, snappily. "They're ugly, vicious brutes, and I don't care to have my two girls exposed to the danger of being bitten."

"I understand that Minna is going alone to the Princess Tchemova's," Portia said, directly, scorning preambles. "I just want to warn you against letting her go there alone, especially at night."

"I'm ashamed of you, Portia Diffardale," rebuked her sister-in-law, with her irritating assumption of superiority. "You're just jealous of the princess and the preference she's shown for mother and me and the girls. The very idea of keeping Minna and Alice away from a charming woman like the princess, who's been so sweet and generous to them! I'm astonished at your petty attitude."

Portia must have groaned within herself at the woman's obtuseness, the inability to recognize a friendly motive on her part.

"I'm sorry that I cannot refute your charge with certain knowledge that I possess, Aurora," she replied coldly. "But the truth is so strange that you would be unlikely to accept it as such, so that I find myself unable to do more than beg you, since you will not listen to my advice, beg you not to let the girls go to the Bumham house alone, especially at night. A policeman disappeared there last evening, Aurora. I tell you, that Russian is a subtle and dangerous woman."

"I don't intend to discuss the matter at all, Portia. You're just plain envious not to be invited to the princess' home as an intimate friend," cried Mrs. Arnold. (I could just imagine her tossing her head, with that air of supercilious triumph.) "I'll thank you, moreover, not to meddle in my affairs any farther. I rather imagine their father and I are able to take care of them perfectly well, without suggestions from you. What do *you* know about a mother's duties and responsibilities, and the necessity of having your children meet the right kind of people socially?"

Well, of course, Portia said no more. She simply took the dogs out, and walked on up the street to give them their much-needed airing. When she came back, it was by way of Queens Boulevard. She noticed the new policeman staring hard at the dogs, and told me that her blood did boil for a moment when she saw the man touch, inadvertently, the pistol at his belt; she couldn't help wondering if perhaps he'd not been given orders to shoot to kill, in case her dogs were found at large without her.

Then she acted on an impulse. She went across to the police signal station, Boris and Andrei walking sedately along on either side of her on their leashes, like the gentlemen they were.

"I just thought I'd make you acquainted with my splendid dogs," she said cheerily. "Boris, shake hands with the officer. Andrei, your paw too, good dog."

"As sure as my name is Murphy, your dogs are real gentlemen," gasped the man amazedly, as the two fine beasts complied with their mistress' order. "Tell me, now, Mrs. Differdale, do you ever let them run out alone at night, about here?"

Portia sensed the inference. That he had called her by name showed that he had been told that it was she who owned the two huge Russian wolfhounds that would permit no one else to approach them unless she were near and gave the command.

"If they are out at night, I am always within call. They are really never out of my sight, even then. And they haven't been running at night for sometime," she finished, pointedly, her eyes straight upon his.

"I'll take your word for it, ma'am. Bedad, they're noble animals," he admired. "It's no harm *they'd* be doing, I'll swear."

Portia was pleased.

"The man knew enough to recognize the truth, in spite of the gossip that had evidently been poured into his ears," she told me afterward.

"Boris and Andrei impressed him as gentlemen, which they are," proudly.

When she left Murphy, it was with the most friendly protestations on his part. Of course, this only made us feel worse later on, when—but again, I'm getting ahead of my story, chronologically.

Owen plucked up sufficient courage that afternoon to telephone Portia, inviting her to take in some play or other in New

York, the following week. She accepted. She did more; she invited Owen to drop in for tea the following afternoon, and when he came, she had marguerites on the tea table and she put a spray of them into his buttonhole and playfully made him promise not to put any other flower there except the ones she gave him. Owen was so overcome at her friendliness that his hand trembled and he nearly dropped the teacup I was passing him.

I could see that he was tremendously excited over the great courtyard (it was his first visit) and the remains of chalked circles and cabalistic signs on the pavement, but he did not mention his interest or curiosity to Portia, although his eyes did seek her face more than once in a puzzled manner. We had a delightful afternoon, and much amusement over Owen's absurd attempts to sit cross-legged like a Turk on a pile of cushions. Portia, of course, had learned to sink gracefully down, and I had practised in private with sufficiently good results to imitate her movements without making too frightful an exhibition of myself.

I was much relieved to see Owen leaving us with Portia's innocent and homely little-sister-to-the-daisy in his buttonhole. But when Owen left the house, the pleasant afternoon we had spent together, the three of us, quite unprepared me for Portia's outburst. She listened until the heavy gate clanged upon his exit, then hid her face in the pile of cushions and broke into such a wild storm of sobs that. I was quite terrified at the shock of the contrast between those paroxysms and her customary cool composure.

"Just let me cry, Auntie," she managed to tell me, when I tried to quiet her. "The storm was due to break, you see, and I can't help thinking how much danger threatens Owen, and how little I can do to shield him. If only I could tell him the truth! But he would be like all the rest. He would think me out of my mind. I wonder that you haven't thought so too, Auntie."

"I don't, my dear, because if your brain isn't all right, mine isn't, either," I admitted. "I've heard and seen so many unsettling things these last days that the more I think on the subject, the more facts seem to pile up and point out one conclusion. Our grocer told me this morning that when the princess told him to make up a list of staples he had included a bag of salt and she had it crossed off, with the observation that she never used salt. Didn't you tell me . .?"

Portia took herself in hand strongly and sat up, wiping her eyes listlessly.

"She won't touch salt, of course, if she's what I suspect. Neither will she eat sweets nor drink cordials of any kind. And she will use quantities of raw meat, unless"—she shuddered—"unless she has found a victim recently. We'll have to find out just what her orders are during the next few days."

I shuddered at that, myself. I couldn't help wondering if the princess had canceled her standing order for raw meat for the time being, or if the same quantity were being delivered. The next time I went downtown, I inquired, and found that *the quantity had been cut down for two days*. It made me sick to think of it. . .

VI

Nothing of any importance happened for the next ten days. Owen became a constant visitor at the house, however. Portia kept a standing order at her florist's for marguerites, and Owen wore one constantly in his buttonhole. (I surmised that there might be an occult significance to the marguerite, but it just happened that I never asked Portia about it).

On the evening that my niece went with Owen to the theater another item was added to the dark list against the Princess Tchemova.

Officer Murphy disappeared from his post sometime during the night, exactly as had his predecessor. But he left no trace behind him; he had apparently vanished into thin air. No one had seen him go. No one knew when he had gone. The fact remained that in the morning the signal station door was open, as if he had only stepped across the road, in sight of the building, but the officer himself was nowhere to be found.

Naturally, there was another furor. I learned the facts when I went down in the morning to do my shopping. When I ordered the chops for dinner, I forced myself to ask, although sick premonition nearly overwhelmed me, if the princess were still ordering such large quantities of meat. Gus remarked that she had telephoned in that morning that she would need *only half the usual quantity* for a couple of days. . . Nausea almost drove me out of the shop.

I learned something more than the authorities were to know, for when I passed the foot of Elm Street, Mrs. Differdale—who was sweeping the sidewalk before her house and evidently watching the boulevard—called to me and beckoned imperatively. I was forced, much against my will, to turn up the street to see what she wanted.

"Come into the house, please, dear Miss Delorme," she murmured with agitation, when I had reached her side. "I've got something to ask you, but I don't want anybody else to hear."

I followed her into the house, feeling that somehow she had stumbled across some fact related to the disappearance of the second policeman.

"I heard somebody say that the new policeman is missing this morning?" she half asserted, half asked. "I'm afraid to tell the authorities what happened last night. Minna said she'd met the princess on the boulevard, and the princess wanted to buy the child some chocolates but had forgotten her purse, so she said she'd send Agathya to buy them that afternoon, and Minna was to go over for them at night."

"Where is Minna?" I almost screamed at Mrs. Differdale. It startled her so that she almost fell backward on the stairway. Her new boudoir cap slipped awry but she did not notice it. A horrible fear was assailing me.

"She's all right. Why, what's the matter?" breathlessly.

"Nothing. Nothing." I could willingly have sunk upon the stairs myself, so great was the reaction at her reply.

"Well," she continued, mysteriously, "when Officer Murphy saw Minna going into the princess' grounds, he called to say that he'd go with her, because it was growing dark. He walked up to the door with her. Minna said the princess seemed awfully put out about something when the child told her how kind the policeman had been. Then all at once she said she'd forgotten the candy, and that Minna must come for it some other time, and that Minna must run right home. She went out to the door with Minna and said something in a low tone to the policeman, who nodded. Then. . ."

"But you are sure that Minna is safe? Where is she now? In school?"

"Why, of course. Where should she be?" wonderingly. "The odd thing is that Minna was the last person to see Murphy alive last night, and I'm afraid to tell the authorities, for fear we'll all be drawn into some court procedure and perhaps the poor child half-frightened to death by legal inquiry into the disappearance."

I saw the drift of her conversation. Mrs. Differdale wanted me to tell her to remain quiet on the subject. I thought concentratedly for a minute. Then I advised her to keep the matter to herself, but to forbid Minna's entering the princess' grounds again after dark, at any rate. Of course, I couldn't give any other reason than the fact that two police officers had disappeared in the vicinity in the course of a couple of weeks, and that it was as well to safeguard the child, even at the cost of losing a box of chocolates, or of offending the Princess Tchemova. I think Mrs. Differdaie was really very glad to have me give her this advice; it must have confirmed her own secret feelings.

I reported the conversation to Portia, who telephoned Owen. She asked him if he had seen the princess that morning. Owen said that she had stopped at his office on her way into town, and had mentioned that she was going to tell the authorities that she had been the last person to see him alive; that he had accompanied Minna Arnold to her door for a box of candy she had promised the child, but which she had forgotten; that she had gone to the door with the child and thanked the officer for looking after the little girl, and had seen the two walk down the path toward the boulevard.

It sounded very frank and straightforward on the princess' part. Still I could see that Portia was thoughtful about it when she related it to me afterward.

"They're putting two officers out here," she told me. "They have orders not to get out of each other's sight. That may help some," significantly.

It was that same morning that Andrei began to show signs of illness. Poor dog! It did not occur to me that the trouble was anything worse than an attack of indigestion or something of that kind, so Fu did not call Portia's attention to the animal until it was too late. The Chinaman found the remains of a large piece of raw meat lying inside the enclosure as if it had been tossed over the wall. When Portia examined it, she turned her face to me, grim and determined.

"Aunt Sophie, somebody has tried to kill my noble dogs. Poor Andrei has been eating poisoned meat. There is only one person interested in eliminating my wolfhounds from the present delicate situation, and you know who that person is. After today, we must keep the dogs inside the house, and watch the enclosure carefully."

The decision to keep the dogs in the house came too late to save Andrei. The poor beast did not suffer long. From the time Fu first observed his drooping behavior until he dropped his white muzzle weakly against Portia's tender hand and drew his last breath, only a couple of hours passed.

Portia was positive that the princess was planning something, and had tried to rid herself of the dogs with some special purpose in view. This made her more than ever careful about Boris, whom we kept with us in the house from then on, or on the leash when we walked outside.

I told Portia that I intended to ask Gus Stieger about how much meat the princess had been buying during those last days. She had, like me, a horrible suspicion, and felt that we must confirm it, although it meant sick disgust and horror to entertain it. When I compared notes with my niece a few days afterward, we found that it was true that for two days after the disappearance of O'Brien and two days after the disappearance of Murphy, the Princess Tchemova had cut down one-half on her usual meat order. It was horrible—horrible!

THE TWO OFFICERS WHO WERE now quartered in the signal station were named Willard and O'Toole. O'Toole was the same man who had come to the house not long before, to make inquiries about the dogs. Portia told me the names of the two new men when she returned after going there to complain of her dog's having been poisoned. O'Toole was much exercised at the thought that anybody could want to kill such splendid animals. He remarked that the previous night he had seen a big black dog racing along with a white one, by the hedge of the Burnham place, and Willard wanted to follow them up a bit, but he had objected.

The two policemen hadn't been three nights in their new station before something happened. Willard was severely torn by a "stray dog"; bitten on his shoulder and arm, after having been knocked down by the animal, which he averred was enormous. O'Toole declared he had seen it also, and that he had come up just in time to save his brother officer from severe maceration by the beast's sharp teeth.

"There were two of them, ma'am," he told me. (I made haste to inquire about Willard as soon as I heard the news from Mike Amadio the next morning.) "Sure, if this was Ireland, I'd be tempted to believe that what I saw weren't dogs, but wolves—and wolves of no pleasant kind," he ended, significantly.

The Irish people have their own peculiar superstitions, thought I to myself, as I carried my telltale face away from O'Toole's sharp eyes. I felt that he knew too much, or suspected too much, of the possibilities in the case, being undoubtedly familiar with Irish traditions and folklore.

Mike Amadio asked me pointblank if Boris had been loose that night. He had seen the big white dog, it appeared. Portia would have felt disturbed at this, but Mike's personal interest in a very good customer was sufficient to persuade him that what he had seen couldn't have been Mrs. Differdale's wolfhound.

Meantime Owen had been rather avoiding the Differdale house, it seemed to me. Mrs. Arnold told me with a sour smile, when I met her one afternoon on the boulevard, that the princess had a fine beau in Owen Edwardes, who was all the time courting her, up at her house when she wasn't down in his office. It made me feel dreadful to tell this to Portia, but of course it had to be done. Portia looked at me, silent suffering in her clouded gaze.

GREYE LA SPINA

"I can't do anything now, Auntie," she said to me; and I knew that it was taking all her self-control not to let herself go in hysterical tears. "There's nothing to be done now, but await developments."

It must have been three weeks after Willard's injury—it had not been sufficient for him to be taken off the beat, and after his wound had been dressed he was back again with O'Toole—when the next act in that tragedy of evil took place. Portia and I had been studying together from certain books—Portia looking up things and reading them to me, and I taking down notes at her dictation—when the telephone rang insistently, and a minute later Fu Sing appeared at the door of the library in an agitation that contrasted ominously with his usual Oriental impassivity.

"Missee, lillee gal go away! No come back!"

Portia sprang up, the books on her lap tumbling to the floor unheeded. "Little girl? What little girl, Fu?"

"Lillee gal Missee Ah-nol."

"Mrs. Arnold's little girl, Portia," I gasped. "Minna!"

My niece and I stared at each other, aghast. Then Portia dashed out of the library and into the hall where the telephone was, and I heard her voice, very clear, very much under control, as she talked to somebody over the wire.

(I ought to state here, that after that day when Portia broke down and cried under the sense of her impotence to aid Owen, she did not again betray such womanly weakness as is shown by tears. I do not remember her crying; she went dry-eyed, tight-lipped, self-controlled, through the terrible things that came to pass before we finally won out of the mists of evil that the dark powers wove about us).

"Officer O'Toole?" she was saying.

I listened, tiptoeing to the door the better to hear every word.

"Yes, this is Mrs. Differdale. Missing? Minna Arnold? Since when? Since half-past eight this evening? Why, it's nearly midnight now! Good God, man, why didn't you call me up before now? What? You didn't think—? You say that Willard saw the child walking up the roadway to the princess' house? And she did not return? This was at eight o'clock? And then you heard her scream? Talk—talk—I'll listen!"

For several minutes my niece held the receiver to her ear, without speaking. Then she said very sharply and decidedly: "Listen, Officer O'Toole. My dog Boris has been lying across my feet all the evening and hasn't been out of sight of Miss Delorme or myself all day, so what you insinuate is utterly impossible. It wasn't Boris you saw. Put that absolutely out of your mind. I shall go over to see Mrs. Arnold right away, and may drop in on my return to see the Princess Tchemova, if you will do me the kindness to accompany me, both of you, to her house."

Her tones indicated deep but controlled feeling, and I could see her lips tighten as she hung up the receiver. She turned to me impulsively.

"Minna went to see the princess at about eight o'clock, Auntie, to get a box of chocolates. At half-past eight Willard heard a child's scream from the princess' grounds, and without waiting for O'Toole to accompany him, he rushed over. In the middle of the boulevard, where it runs past the princess' house, he found a broken box of expensive chocolates spilled all over the street. Nothing more. By this time O'Toole had joined him. He told O'Toole that he had seen a white wolfhound dashing away through the princess' grounds. They went up to the house together, and were told that the princess had retired for the night with a severe headache. Sergei opened the door to them. He said the child had called for the candy, which he had given her at the princess' orders. He knew nothing more about the matter, but said he thought he had heard someone scream, out on the boulevard."

Portia's eyes sought mine, fall of a terrible significance.

"You really believe, then," I stammered, "that she—?"

"I believe, Aunt Sophie, that the princess couldn't appear because she was unable to show herself in her metamorphosed form," she replied grimly.

"What are you going to do, my dear?"

"I must go to see poor Aurora first. Then I must also call at the house of the Princess Tchernova," decidedly.

"Portia! Take care, my dear girl!"

I was terrified, as I might well be. To walk into that den of devils, where she could only expect the worst at their hands. . .

"I shall take Boris on the leash," she went on calmly. "Don't be afraid that anything will happen to me, Auntie dear. Nothing could possibly happen tonight, because of what has just happened to Minna. The most savage wild beast will not attack when it has eaten its fill."

She shuddered, and for a moment covered her eyes with one hand.

"I'm hoping that I may be in time—to save that poor little creature—but I'm afraid it will be too late."

I wanted to go with her, but she refused decidedly to let me venture out. She declared so positively that she would be safe that I was obliged to take her word for it.

"Don't you see, Auntie, that she wouldn't dare do more tonight, without throwing suspicion upon herself? As it is, they've tried to make it appear that Minna was abducted on her way home. Automobiles are passing every minute on the boulevard. And the broken box of chocolates in the middle of the road! O'Toole thought at once of an abduction."

Portia was ready for the street in a very short time. I called up Owen in the meantime, and he was waiting outside in his car by the time she was ready. She had changed her mind about taking Boris; she did not need the dog if she had Owen with her, she said. She left the house about midnight. It was half past I when she returned.

I was waiting for her in the library, devouring page after page from the strange books she had taken out for me to study.

Owen would not come in, because it was so late.

PART III

I

Portia flung herself down upon the cushions near me, her eyes blazing with that somber light so unlike her usual gentle expression.

"Oh, it seems incredible! And yet—even the most skeptical would have to believe, after learning what I have learned. I must work hard from now on, or that fiend in human form will have gotten the best of us all—and that house will have become a veritable shambles. Ugh!"

"And Owen?"

She turned melting eyes upon me; her lips quivered until she drew them firmly together into a straight line.

"Owen, Auntie? Oh, he must be the least in my thoughts, Owen whom I love! It may be that I shall be called upon to sacrifice even Owen, to save others for whom I care nothing!"

"Portia! Sacrifice Owen?"

"Auntie, to snare that ancient evil I may be obliged to permit Owen to walk into her net. That's what I mean. Don't think I want to do it. God knows I don't. But God knows, too, that from now on my life is dedicated to this one thing, to thwart and balk the evil that lives in the white body of the Russian woman."

I dared not speak. Despite my fluttering doubts, my spirit of modern incredulity, I had come to accept Portia's great knowledge of the ancient mysteries, of the old-time occultism, as matters of fact. There was much that I could not understand then; yet I believed, if not in the things of themselves, in Portia's knowledge and her belief in them. I knew, intuitively, that my niece was not out of her head; I knew that she had mastered deep truths, on the dim verge of knowing which I was still shrinking, out of terror at what I felt full acceptance and belief would bring upon my soul. So I remained silent, but ready to acquiesce in whatever Portia should propose.

I think she sensed my feeling, for she looked at me all at once, and a smile that came close upon tears passed over her sweet face. She put out one hand, laying it on mine.

"I must not let my emotions master me, Auntie. I must be very, very strong. It is when we permit our feelings to get the better of our minds that we become weak and lose our grip on things. And now—"—(she changed her gentle tones for others more brisk)—"I suppose you want to know all about my visits tonight?"

It had been too late, she told me, to save Minna Arnold. The terrified and grief-stricken mother had promised, however, not to let Alice out of her sight after dark, and especially not to let her go across the boulevard alone, or to the house of the princess, if unaccompanied.

"She doesn't understand, of course, why I laid so much stress on the latter point," Portia said wearily, "but it isn't necessary for her to understand, if she will only keep her word to me."

THE STORY WAS GOING THE rounds that Minna had been kidnapped on her return from the princess' residence. It was better so, of course. Willard and O'Toole would not, after all, swear to the white wolfhound, although in private Willard told Portia he was quite sure he had seen Agathya's stooping figure run across the road and into the shrubbery about the princess' grounds, as the two officers approached. This might have been an optical illusion, Willard admitted, and when Portia asked him not to mention it, he agreed readily, remarking that there was something uncanny about the whole business, and that the sooner he could be transferred to another beat, the better pleased he'd be. He said he couldn't forget the glowing red eyes of the white hound that had chewed his shoulder, and he was sure it hadn't been Boris or Andrei.

"About my visit to the princess, Auntie. Sergei managed to make me understand in broken English, and by signs, that she could not be seen, as she had retired early with a sleeping potion beeause of a headache. This is what he also managed to make O'Toole understand. Agathya— oh, that Russian woman isn't human!—She's a fiend! I can reconstruct that whole business now, Auntie.

"The princess ordered Agathya to drag Minna into the house when the child came to the door. Agathya, fearing to become a victim herself unless she obeyed her mistress, implicitly did as she was ordered. Then she took the chocolates down to the boulevard and scattered them over the road, and when that was done, she screamed, once. Then she rushed back and hid. And meantime—"—(she shuddered, but controlled herself quickly)— "meantime, the princess in her metamorphosed state dragged the wretched child down into the basement—"

"Portia, that is too much! I can't believe it! It's too horrible! It's too incredible!" I groaned.

"Poor Auntie, I don't blame you. But it's only too true."

I recovered myself somewhat. "Go on, Portia," I said.

"Agathya, I believe, refused to be a party to the murder of that child. I imagine she has rebelled from time to time and has had to suffer accordingly until she was bent to her mistress' wicked will."

"Portia—it's awful!"

"She was lying on the cushions in the great salon, Auntie. I pushed my way in, although Sergei tried to prevent me. Agathya lifted those terribly pathetic dog's-eyes to my face, turned her head to Sergei with fear written on her countenance, mingled with determination, then with a sudden motion pulled down her dress from her shoulders and disclosed bleeding welts—all raw—from the blows of a knout! Oh, you may shudder and shrink, Auntie; it turned me sick, I can tell you."

"What did Sergei do then?" I was trembling as I asked.

"He came across the room and drew her dress gently up into place over her shoulders. Then he pointed to the door and looked me straight in the eyes, with a gesture of resignation. I bent down and caressed that poor, broken creature at my feet. Sergei had said nothing, but I understood; my stay would only make it harder for Agathya. I went at once."

"But how did you find out about Minna?" My shudders shook me uncontrollably.

"Sergei made me understand. He knows very little English, but he told me plainly enough with what he knew, by combining it with gestures."

"And you believed?" I reproached her.

"Yes, Auntie, I realized that I was too late. You see, I told him at once that I knew what the princess was. '*Volkodlak*', he repeated after me, his eyes aflame. Then he beat his hands upon his breast, repeating over and over, 'Sergei—love—*volkodlak*.'"

"Oh, how can he? A fiend like that!"

"Love doesn't go where it's commanded, Auntie," Portia reminded me sadly. "When he saw that I understood what he wanted to convey to me, he picked up—oh, Auntie, Auntie!—A glove that lay on the mantel over the fireplace—a man's glove that I knew, because I had mended a little rip in it one afternoon a few weeks ago—and as he showed it to me, with a fierceness in his eyes that told of his burning, implacable jealousy—'Ow-een,' he said to me. 'Ow-een— *volkodlak*!' Then I came away quickly, because I could not contain myself any longer, and I had to see someone who was good and gentle and self-sustained, like you, Auntie."

"Owen, a werewolf? No, no, I don't believe it!" I cried out in vehement denial.

Portia spoke again, after a moment's silence.

"Agathya is dumb," she said, as if irrelevantly. "Her tongue is out. She had to be made a safe servant for such a dangerous mistress."

I began to sob dryly. I couldn't control my nervous shudders. The thought that the world held such demons at large was too much for me. Portia let me sob in silence for a few minutes; then she suggested that I let her give me a sleeping potion that would insure sound, dreamless slumber.

She came into my room when I was ready for bed, and brought me a glassful of what seemed to be a delicious raspberry vinegar, but, innocuous though it appeared, it made me sleep more soundly than I can remember having slept for years; the moment my head touched the pillow I was asleep, and I did not waken until nearly ten o'clock the following day, when I found myself refreshed wonderfully and prepared to face almost anything.

I may as well remark here, that when I wakened in the morning, my so-called "common sense" had once more taken command of my mind, and I thought of my credulity of the previous night with rather a pained smile. I have read since that psychic researchers often find that what impresses them deeply when they are in the midst of their psychic work loses its depth and significance after the passing of a few hours of commonplace life. It was so with me. I waked with a clear head, and the thought that poor Minna had been kidnapped, and that Portia's talk with me was nothing but part of a strange dream.

OWEN EDWARDES HAD CALLED UP about nine o'clock. Portia told me. She came in when she heard me stirring about. Owen had had a message from the princess, who had sent for him at once upon hearing the news from her servants in the morning. She had begged him to tell the police that she was shocked to have had such a thing happen to the child on its way back from her house, and wished to offer a reward of a thousand dollars for news leading to the recovery of the kidnapped child.

Owen was very enthusiastic about the princess' kindly interest. He added that of course she was in no wise to blame for the unhappy occurrence, but that she kept blaming herself for having asked the child to come for the candy at night. Portia repeated the conversation, without letting her own knowledge, or her own feelings, tinge the recital of Owen's message.

The princess had asked him to thank Mrs. Differdale for her call on the night before, and regretted that her headache had incapacitated her for receiving unexpected callers! Portia did not think that either Sergei or Agathya had told their mistress of her visit; she imagined that Owen had let the fact drop unintentionally (he had accompanied her to the door that night), or else the princess had been cognizant of what was passing between her servants and Portia.

I thought it very decent of the princess, at least, to offer a reward for the kidnapers of Minna. You see, my "common sense" was ruling my mind for the moment.

"Very decent," said Portia.

I felt something intangibly critical in her tone, but while I wanted to tell her that we'd both been incredibly silly in our surmises the preceding night, she gave me no opportunity. Afterward I knew that she was perfectly aware of the fading of psychic impressions with the passage of a few hours, so she alertly avoided an argument.

It must have been just before lunchtime that I heard a siren outside and looked from my upper window over the wall to see the limousine of the Princess Tchernova standing before the house. Sergei got down from the seat, but he did not open the car door as I expected; instead, he came directly toward our wall and disappeared in the shadow. A moment later, the bell pealed.

I was much excited. What message could the princess be sending to us? I heard Fu speak to Portia, who was in the library with Boris, and presently I heard the Chinaman usher Sergei into my niece's presence. I could no more refrain from listening than from eating; the visit was unprecedented and I felt that it meant something more than a mere visit. Was Sergei bringing a message, or had he come on his own account? I was soon to learn, but not from his impassioned exclamations that came, disjointed and incoherent, drifting through the open library door. I was obliged to wait until Fu had opened the bronze gate and let the chauffeur out again. Then I rushed into the library.

"Portia, what has happened now?" I demanded.

Portia was lying back on the cushions, looking very white but very determined.

"The Princess Tehernova has definitely determined to effect Owen's metamorphosis," she said simply, with what for the moment appeared to me to be an entire lack of feeling, but that I realized afterward was due to strong self-control, forced upon her by the terrible responsibility now resting on her shoulders.

"Portia! Are you crazy?"

"'Why, no, Auntie. I'm rather more than ordinarily calm and well balanced," responded my niece. Only her hands, clenched into white-knuckled fists with the intensity of her emotion, betrayed any feeling.

"But, Portia—what are you trying to tell me? It's absurd, ridiculous!" I blustered, suddenly losing all the calm poise with which I had wakened that morning.

"Neither absurd nor ridiculous, Auntie, but very, very real—and very, very terrible!"

"What—what are you going to do about it, Portia?" I faltered. All my lofty common sense had deserted me. I found myself shrinking with the same awful feeling of impotence that I had experienced the night before during my niece's recital of the monstrous things that had happened.

Portia got up out of her cushions slowly. Her eyes were distant, and she did not look directly at me. Her voice sounded as if it came from afar, so little did it appear to issue from her hardly parted lips.

"I must get to work," she said in that faraway manner, as if she were not speaking to me but to someone else, very distant.

"To work?" I cried out. "But aren't you going to warn Owen?"

"To warn him? Oh, I'm going to do more than warn him. I'm going to try to save him if that is humanly—or superhumanly—possible. He wouldn't listen to my warnings, Aunt Sophie. He's under that woman's influence now. I've seen it for days. He—he's not been wearing the flowers I sent him. He's broken his word, and he's been wearing those hideous orchids of hers. He's been dining with her almost every night for the past week. She's been gradually drawing him into her net."

"If you're afraid to warn him, let me!" I cried, rather wildly, and with more than a hint of reproach, I fear.

She fixed me with a cold smile.

"Do you really flatter yourself that Owen would listen to what you'd try to tell him. Aunt Sophie, when you hardly know what the truth of the matter is, yourself?" She turned to leave the room. "Better leave things in my hands, dear," she said, more gently.

"Or in God's," I supplemented, rebukingly.

"Yes—in God's," she murmured, lifting her eyes upward as if in silent invocation.

"Why did Sergei tell you about all this?" I demanded.

"Sergei loves the princess. She had promised him that some day his faithful, unquestioned love was to be rewarded. Now he suspects that instead of making him her wolf-mate, she has determined to have Owen. His furious jealousy—oh, he is a man of strong passions!— has been aroused, and he wishes me to interfere—to save Owen, he said, but what he really wishes is my interference, to clear his own path. He tells me that the princess has been trying to administer her strange drinks to Owen during this past week, but that he—Sergei has managed once or twice to change the glasses. Not out of consideration for Owen, understand. Sergei would care little if Owen died at the princess' hands during her metamorphosis. It is Owen's life—and Owen's metamorphosis—that Sergei is fighting against."

"And Owen has lent himself to this—this evil experiment?"

"Owen, Sergei tells me, has been reluctant and indifferent to the princess' wiles, but the evil spells are digging their way into his soul. One must flee evil, never stop to play with it. And then, there will be a special conjunction of certain planets in a few nights, with Saturn in the ascendant."

" What has that to do with it?"

She turned from me, saying over her shoulder: "Much, that would take too long to explain. Don't disturb me, dear, will you, until I come to you again? I shall be at work in the laboratory. There is much to do. and only God knows what the outcome of this tragic tangle will be."

"You're not going to—to make incantations—and that kind of thing?" In that moment, I was frankly afraid for her, thinking of her husband's

"Auntie, I shall probably make several very dangerous experiments. It is for this that I beg you not to disturb me. Any disturbance might end fatally for me," she warned me gravely.

I promised.

II

Fu carried dinner into the laboratory, but Portia refused it, he told me. Fu was worried about her, but confident in her wisdom.

"Missee make big magic," he told me mysteriously, when I looked disturbedly at the untouched tray.

His smile restored something of my lost, tranquillity; if Fu could feel proud and pleased and satisfied at what his mistress was undertaking, then Portia's aunt ought to have a little faith in her, also.

"Missee no can eat now," Fu assured me, with pleased gravity; "bimeby, missee eat. No can make magic if missee eat."

I caught at his meaning then. One drew nearer, Portia had told me, to the spiritual world, when one banished one's consciousness of the body. That is the reason that so many religious sects lay stress upon the mortification of the flesh. Portia did not believe in mortification of the flesh, but she did believe in mastering it. I realized that she was not eating because she did not wish at this crucial juncture to center her thoughts upon anything less than the highest on the spiritual plane. I lost my disturbed feeling and felt a sudden influx of trust and confidence in my niece. Portia knew what she was doing; she had not been Mr. Differdale's pupil and helper for nothing. If there was something wrong going on—and I knew—there must be much beneath the surface—Portia understood how to meet that evil with the good that must always conquer, else the world would fall.

I waited, therefore, with what patience I could summon, for my niece to emerge from the laboratory to give me whatever instructions I might need to assist her in saving Owen from the clutches of an evil before which I knew myself, with my limited knowledge of the occult, as helpless as a child. My mind was full of surmises. I thought of the passionate and jealous Sergei, and of the broken, shrinking Agathya with her frightened doglike eyes; I thought of that incarnation of evil beauty called the Princess Irma Tchemova. And last of all, but not least, I thought long of Owen, of the danger in which he stood, and which he so little realized. And after I had thought and thought, without finding any conclusion to my thoughts, I just slipped down upon my knees and prayed softly and earnestly.

It was while I was praying that Portia came into the library, putting her hand on my shoulder gently as if she was sorry to disturb me. I got up and met her eyes, half-ashamed of this disclosure of my inmost self: the soul does not care to be found at its secret devotions. She met my gaze with a kind of proud humility, as if she understood my helplessness, my involuntary confession that I, as a mere human being, was at a loss. I knew when I met her clear gaze that she had learned how to deal with conditions and circumstances before which I, with so many more years of worldly experience, was helpless.

She was dressed in her simple laboratory apron, but there was about her a kind of light that shone through, as if it permeated her entire body and glowed in each cell. It was soft and beautiful, and I felt all at once that she had found something for which I had been seeking ardently for years, something for which the whole world is searching with deep spiritual hunger. I wanted to get nearer to her, to touch her reverently, but at the same time something intangible in her atmosphere kept me at a little distance. I waited for her to speak; I felt that it was not for me to offer suggestions, but for her to give orders that I must obey implicitly, without question.

"Auntie, dear." She spoke with a kind of childish appeal.

I waited expectantly.

"Auntie, I've been at the Princess Tehemova's this evening."

"What?" I cried out in consternation. "Fu told me that you had been shut up all afternoon and evening in the laboratory."

"Well—I was."

"But you just said—?"

"It was my body that was shut up in the laboratory, Auntie. How stupid of me not to think—! You see, I—oh, it's very hard to explain, when you have never read or studied anything about it, Aunt Sophie. Mr. Differdale taught me how to project the astral body consciously—"

"What?"

Well, it was a long explanation and a hard one, and finally Portia had to ask me to take her word for it that it was possible to separate what St. Paul calls "the body and the spirit." I believe he said there was a "fleshly body and a spiritual body," and what I understood from Portia was, that she had learned how to disentangle her spiritual body from her fleshly body, and to travel wherever she chose in that spiritual, or astral body. Of course, it was a new thing to me, consequently hard to understand; I don't fully understand it, even now. But I told her at last to go ahead with whatever she had learned, while away in her astral body; that I'd try to understand.

SHE SAID SHE'D BEEN INSIDE the Princess Tchemova's house, invisible, unheard. The princess was giving a special dinner for Owen. Owen had been wearing a strange red flower in his buttonhole, a flower that resembled an ox-eye daisy, but with a thick, fleshy stem and a faint, sickish odor. The whole dining room was crowded with marigolds, azaleas, and lilies of the valley, and the heavy combined scent hung stagnant upon the close air. The fragrance that Owen had once considered disagreeable, he was now indifferent to, for when the princess broke off a marigold and offered it to him with a searching look, he took the odorous yellow bloom and held it to his nostrils almost with enjoyment.

Then the princess had lifted an embroidered linen cloth from a tabouret and had taken up two woven chains of those hideously loathsome growths that she called orchids. One she placed about her own neck, where it swung nearly to her knees; the other she flung about the neck of her favored guest.

"She has bewitched Owen, Auntie. He doesn't realize what it all means. He—he even kissed her hand—that terrible hand!—When she stretched it out to him like a queen to a captive slave. And then she flung herself into his arms and told him that she loved him with a reckless passion, and that the stars had marked him out as her future lover, her future husband. Oh, it was cruelly hard to see and hear all this, and know that for the time being I could do nothing!"

She continued in her story, with a calmness that I envied her. I felt that she was being buoyed up by something which she had not yet told me, and all I could do was to wait with impatience.

Owen had kissed the princess' slim hand—and then he began to reach for her red lips, always with a kind of strange apathy—but then she pushed him gently away and led him to the table, where stood a great flagon of that strangely sparkling water, to drink which means the doom of a man's soul under the curse of lycanthropy. She poured out two brimming goblets and offered him one while she drained the other, in symbol of their coming marriage, which she averred should be celebrated in real Russian fashion.

A circle of seven feet in diameter and another of three feet within the first, she drew with a bit of chalk and a long cord. In the central circle she placed a brazier over which swung a pot with some spring water and certain herbs (the names of these Portia observed were in her books and therefore unnecessary to enumerate, and I particularly refrain now from writing them down, for the reason that those who knew, know; and those who do not and want to, probably ought not to know). The princess made certain passes about Owen, who remained as if hypnotized, his eyes fixed upon his enchantress. Then when the liquid boiled, she dipped a branch of parsley into it, and flung the hot decoction dripping over him, crying aloud certain words in Russian as she did so.

At that, Portia's concentrated strength of will deserted her; she could no longer contain her emotion. She tried to throw herself between that embodied evil and that man who was loved to his own doom, and found herself waking back in her home, merged once more into the heavy body of flesh from which for a short time she had contrived to free herself.

"How could you bear it?" I cried to her then. "How can you stand here and tell me all this so calmly? Is your heart a piece of ice, Portia?"

"No, not ice, Auntie. You see, I am trusting in higher powers than those powers of evil. I have—an assurance—that everything will come out right. We must be patient. Tomorrow, when I can manage to get in touch with Owen, I shall have him come here, and then I shall take the necessary steps—"

"Then you know how to free him from the spell?"

"I know what can be attempted, dear. But the outcome is always on the knees of the gods."

A long, rushing sound all at once swelled out, filling our ears with ominous, rumbling thunder. I caught at Portia's arm in terror.

"What is that?"

Her great, serious eyes dilated. Her other hand went involuntarily to her breast as if to quiet the beating of her heart. And then came the explosion. We were rooted to the spot with the awful terror of that unknown catastrophe.

"Missee! Missee! Plincess house go to the sky!"

It was Fu who came running to apprise us of the thing that had happened. We ran upstairs without need of touching the electric switch that controlled the hall lights, for a blaze of red and yellow poured through the windows, announcing the catastrophe before we could see it. From the windows of Portia's room, which faced the west, we two women saw the tremendous volume of flame and billowing black smoke that roared and swirled skyward from what had been the old Burnham house; then we turned our pallid faces to each other.

"Better so, Portia, my own dear girl! Better so—than that other!" I cried out.

Portia gave a little moan, and stepped back weakly against my outstretched arms. I folded her closely to me. It was, after all, for the best. If what she had told me was true, it was far, far better that Owen should have died suddenly in that explosion than that he should have lived under the curse of lycanthropy, and at the beck and call of that evil thing that possessed and animated the body of the Russian princess.

Portia stirred in my arms finally, at the sound that came loudly across the fields, of fire-engines with their clanging and their sirens. She put me gently aside and once more turned to look from the window. For a few minutes she stood there without speaking, her eyes fixed on that blazing funeral pyre. Then she drew a long breath, lifting her eyes upward as if in search of power to resign herself to the inevitable.

"I'm going down into the laboratory," she began, when I clutched at her again, nervously. The gate-bell had rung loudly, an alarm that conveyed a sense of agitation to my jangled nerves.

She sprang away from my extended hand and went down the hall, down the stairway, before I could gather my scattered wits sufficiently to follow. Then I heard her cry out.

"Agathya!" And then, "No! No!

Owen! Owen!"

NOTWITHSTANDING MY AGE AND MY clinging skirts, I managed to get to the top of the staircase in double-quick time. I looked down. At the foot of the stairs stood Agathya, holding a great gray dog on a leash. Kneeling on the floor, arms about the beast's neck, was my niece Portia, uttering little cries whose import I could not understand. Agathya, I could see, had been crying; her face was streaked with tears, and her eyes were red and swollen. What had brought her here? Why the gray dog? I hurried down.

"Owen has been saved!" cried Portia.

I knew that she was addressing me, although she did not rise from her knees, and continued to caress the gray dog that stood passively as if frightened.

"Where is he?" I looked about but did not see him.

And then the dumb Agathya pointed, her trembling finger indicating—. Why, no, it was impossible! The gray dog—! Was it a dog? Was it not, rather—?

Then I screamed.

"Portia! Let it alone! Getaway from it! Let it alone! It isn't a dog!" My voice rose to a frantic shriek. "It's—a—wolf!"

Portia did not rise. She continued to stroke the beast's head behind the ears that pricked slightly forward as if the animal were listening, puzzled, to our conversation.

"I know what it is, Auntie. Don't frighten it, please. It isn't really a wolf. It is—Owen!"

And at that plain statement I understood. But the understanding was too much for me. The blood rushed hotly up into my head; I felt blackness swooping down upon me from every side. I clutched dizzily at the stair-rail.

"Oh! So—it—is—Owen!" I heard my voice saying, as if from some great distance. Then I knew no more.

When I came back to consciousness, I was lying on my own cushions in my own room, and Agathya was squatting on the floor beside me. The old woman was crying softly and plaintively.

III

Although it was not for days afterward that I myself learned the story of Owen's metamorphosis, and the fate of the Princess Irma Tchernova and her devoted chauffeur, chronologically it ought to have gone into this recital of acts before Portia and I stood at the window that night, watching the holocaust of what had been one of the fine old landmarks of Meadowlawn. Agathya's inability to speak even her native language might have proved a serious impediment to our acquiring knowledge of what took place at the old Burnham house before the explosion, had not the old woman been fairly gifted with her pencil in the manner of crude drawings, and had she not possessed sufficient histrionic ability to combine with those rough sketches. Her own system for conveying ideas to her mistress or Sergei helped us but little.

Afterward, she partly drew, partly acted out, the happenings of that night, until Portia and I understood very well what had taken place. Her story was fully corroborated from Owen's angle, later, although his recollection of what took place was dim, as if his mind had not been absolutely clear at the time. It would be entirely too tedious if I tried to tell the whole story of Agathya's attempts to impart her knowledge of that last terrible night, and I think it will be better if I tell it as if I had witnessed the whole tragedy in person.

Agathya managed to make us understand that she had been foster-mother to the princess when Irma was a baby, hence something more than a serf, but that Irma had always treated her nurse as an unscrupulous person is likely to treat a person who loves one. It was not until Irma had gone far in the ways of evil knowledge that Agathya lost her tongue, and she lost it because she had seen fit to rebuke her mistress for cruel treatment of some small animal upon which the princess had been making experiments. The princess' retaliation for this reproach was frightful, but it meant Agathya's future silence, and Agathya's shrinking, fearful service from that time on. What Irma Tchemova failed to understand was that some day her ancient servitor would turn upon such a tyrannical mistress, her love changed to implacable hatred.

When the princess had completed the experiments in black magic that made it possible for her to metamorphose at will, she had yet another hold upon her terrified old nurse; she told Agathya that if she could not find victims upon whom to glut her appetite for human flesh, she would rend the old woman limb from limb in lieu of other prey. This threat was sufficient in itself to bind the broken-spirited Agathya, who no longer dared oppose her mistress in anything.

This condition was taken full advantage of by the princess, who often slaked her thirst for blood, when she was angry, by forcing Agathya to bare her back to the knout, which the Russian would wield until crimson followed her blows. Sometimes after this she would relent, and weep, begging her old nurse's pardon. This had taken place several times, and Agathya alternately found herself swayed between her old love for her one-time foster-child, and her cringing fear of the terrible beatings she might expect to receive upon what was too often a slight provocation.

ON THE NIGHT OF THE fire, Agathya had received orders to prepare a more than ordinarily splendid dinner. The heavy brocaded draperies were drawn close across the windows by the hands of the princess herself, intent upon privacy. Irma dressed with more than her customary attention, decking herself with many-colored jeweled ornaments to accentuate her exotic beauty. She wore a corsage bouquet of lycanthropic flowers of various colors, ranging from the deep orange with puffy black blotches, to sickly white or palish blue or ugly garnet. The brazier, of which Portia had told me, was prepared, and its contents carefully measured, ready for use in the incantations. The wreaths or chains of those terrible "orchids" were tied together by the princess' own slender fingers and laid under an embroidered linen cover on a small table in the dining room.

Agathya had her suspicions as to the event that her mistress was preparing for, and when Sergei, attired for the affair with barbaric splendor in robes of rich embroidery after the ancient Russian fashion, appeared in the kitchen to see to the final arrangements, the old woman inquired of her fellow-servant by means of deaf-and-dumb signs if the guest were not to be Owen Edwardes, and if the occasion were not to be Owen's initiation into the lycanthropic rites that would result in his metamorphosis. It was a matter not to be ignored between Sergei and Agathya, for the old woman knew how madly the chauffeur loved his mistress; knew that he had followed the princess chiefly because of his wild passion, not because he had been born to service, for it seems that in Russia he had been a small nobleman.

"Tonight the princess intends to make Ow-een her mate," he marled between shut teeth. "Yes, tonight she will make a grand foray somewhere in the neighborhood, with a partner, a mate, at her side. She wishes to glut her hunger in company with the man whom she loves. Well, she reckons without me. She has lied to me once too often, Agathya."

He laughed. It made Agathya shudder, for it was a fearful sound, mirthless and grim, that issued from his lips.

"Tonight is to be her night of love. It shall be! It shall be such love as that pale American could never dream of. Even our princess does not know of the love that is in store for her tonight. Oh, my time has come. I shall wait no longer. She shall be mine—or no man's."

"What are you going to do?" Agathya's nimble fingers demanded, while the old woman's eyes dilated with apprehension for her fellow-servant, who had more than once saved her from the princess' knout. "If you offend her, your chance to win her for yourself will be gone forever. This may be only a passing fancy for the American."

"A passing fancy? When she intends to make him her lycanthropic mate?" Sergei demanded savagely. "Tonight she will either make me her wolf-mate or slay that interloper when she metamorphoses. I have waited too long. My patience is exhausted. The hour has come when I must act."

Agathya trembled. "Why should she kill that poor young man?" she questioned. Agathya was afflicted by pity for Owen, and sympathy for Portia, who had once laid a gentle hand upon that wounded shoulder.

Sergei stared at the old woman.

"If the princess chooses me, then I will spare the young man. If you want his life, Agathya, it is yours, provided only that the American woman takes him away from here, If the princess will not fulfill her promises to me—tonight—" . . .

His unspoken words conveyed to Agathya eloquently all that his lips did not utter.

THE OLD WOMAN WENT ON with her dinner preparations, and Sergei with his dignified serving when dinner was ready. But when the table had been cleared and the princess was left alone with Owen, Sergei was not outside the door; Sergei was standing within the room, behind the heavy draperies near the door, which he had closed cunningly, as he concealed himself. And Sergei's hand was on the hilt of his keen-bladed knife, the knife with the enameled Russian hilt that had looked so colorful against his dark mantle.

What Portia had seen, Sergei saw, with the difference that when the princess flung over Owen the hot drops of the decoction from the pot that hung over the brazier, Sergei saw the thing take place that to him meant Irma Tchemova's betrayal of himself, her acceptance of another man as her mate. Sergei saw the metamorphosis of Owen Edwardes take place before his furious eyes; saw all—all. He was not horrified; he had known for years that the princess was subject to this supernormal change. What he felt was bitter anger at her betrayal of him, furious jealousy at that signal instance of her favor for Owen, and a powerful desire for revenge upon that lovely, lying creature who had beguiled another and innocent man by her magical arts.

The gray wolf that stood within the double circle beside the glowing brazier trembled as if with fright. Sergei read the creature's mood and disposition aright, and a sudden impulse arose within him to snatch the unfortunate beast out of the triumphant princess' power, before that gray muzzle should be stained with innocent blood. His opportunity was not long in coming. For a moment the beautiful Russian stood caressing the rough gray hide of the beast beside her, with incoherent endearments, and an occasional passionate kiss. Then she lifted both slender arms in invocation. As she raised her face upward, Sergei snatched off his long girdle and knotted one end into a running noose.

Very quietly he tiptoed up behind the princess. He dropped the noose about the gray wolf's neck and pulled the animal toward the door. It was all done so quickly—and the beast went with him as if it understood—that when the princess heard the first sound and whirled about, it was too late for her to change the invocation she had already made. That white face was growing elongated—those beryl eyes gleamed with garnet fires—as Sergei pulled the gray wolf out into the hall and closed the door behind him.

He called to the old nurse, who was crouching near the door.

"Here!" He put the knotted girdle into the old woman's trembling hand. "Here is the man you wanted to save. Take him to the American woman who loves him. Do not be afraid. Our mistress will not be able to harm you from now on. I am master, Agathya."

Agathya remained rooted to the spot, her terrified mouth agape. She was unable to question Sergei by her own methods, for her hands were busy with the gray wolf that had been delivered into her keeping. She could only stand, staring, petrified.

"Go! And go quickly!" commanded Sergei, authoritatively. "Already our mistress has changed her form, and she must not find you are here, with this beast—so. Do not think of me. I shall be able to take care both of myself—and her. Go!"

Agathya, accustomed throughout her sixty-odd years to unquestioning obedience, trudged out of the house, drawing the trembling gray wolf with her. She admitted when telling her story that she did not once entertain a fear of the animal, knowing it as she did for a kindly and well-intentioned human being before its metamorphosis. She had been afraid of her mistress when the princess changed her form, and usually kept to her room at night, warned to do so, "in case of accident," as Irma had dryly remarked.

Agathya, however, could not force herself to go away immediately across the fields to the Differdale house, without seeing for herself—if she could do so in safety—what was taking place between her mistress and the enraged Sergei. Therefore, when she had closed the house door securely behind her, she dragged the unwilling beast along with her to where she could peer in at the high windows of the dining room. She found a place at last, where the princess' hand had not drawn the curtains together sufficiently, or where Sergei had disarranged them later inadvertently.

Through the panes her white face peered. At the end of the improvised leash the unwilling beast tugged and strained. Agathya was really terrified beyond expression at her realization that conditions had gone entirely beyond the Princess Tchemova's control and had passed into the hands of the rebellious Sergei. She stood staring into the room, terror in her heart at what she felt intuitively was about to take place, for she knew that the princess would not overlook Sergei's interference.

WITHIN THE BRILLIANTLY LIGHTED SALON there paced back and forth a great white wolf, an animal that the old woman knew only too well. The bushy tail switched angrily. The great beast leapt, and flung itself furiously at the closed door once, twice, then fumbled at the knob with paws and mouth; a horrifying sight, somehow, even to Agathya. At last it gave up, walked back to the center of the room and crouched, facing the

Presently that watched door opened cautiously, to admit Sergei, who closed it quickly behind him and with his back against it, his intention clarified by that simple action. The white wolf drew back with a suspicious snarl. It must have seen, as did Agathya, the glittering, keen-bladed knife that shone in the chauffeur's right hand. Apparently the wolf was uncertain what to do; it stood, lashing its furry sides with its tail, eying Sergei with glowing red eyes that were terrible to see.

"You promised me, Irma Andreyevna!" cried out Sergei finally, with concentrated passion. "You lied to me, didn't you? You were always lying to me, because your promises bound me to your service. Well, you've lied once too often, Irma Andreyevna. You promised me to perform the incantations over me that would make me your mate—but now you have thrust me to one side to make place for that pale American, who does not love you—who does not love you, princess! No, what he gives is only the reflection of your own abandoned, mad passion, an echo of your magic arts drawn out of him in response to your desire.

"You thought you could play with Sergei's heart, didn't you? Ah, you didn't know Sergei as well as you thought you did! You've played with him for the last time. You've told him your last lie. You are going to keep your promises tonight, and lie on Sergei's breast—alive or dead! And he laughed.

At that laugh, a low growl rippled out of the parted jaws of the white wolf. The red eyes glowed savagely. It swayed from side to side, then crouched with tense muscles.

Sergei braced himself against the door, the knife in his hand flashing back the light of the cut-glass pendants of the chandelier. There was a sudden eclipse of the lights, as a long, lithe body intervened between Agathya's staring eyes and the chandelier, in a curving spring. Sergei cried out, as if taken by surprise, flinging his right hand into the air. The knife flashed in that upward sweep.

In her tense condition, Agathya could have sworn that she heard the loud snap of the white wolf's teeth as they met in the empty air, and she breathed in relief, a relief that a second later turned into agonized suspense—for which of the two within she herself could hardly have told. Remember, Agathya had nursed at her own breast the thing that raged within that room. It was truly a horrid sound, followed by a kind of gasping, choking, husky laugh—if laugh it could be called—from Sergei.

Agathya looked. Looked again, hardly believing her own eyes. Sergei was holding the white wolf's ugly snapping jaws close to his bleeding breast, as if in an ecstasy. His mouth was wide open, his head lifted as if he felt an emotion too deep even for joy. He panted as he pressed the bared, red-stained fangs against his very heart with his muscular left arm.

"I told you—you are lying on my heart—my bleeding heart—alive—my princess—alive!"

He raised the knife yet higher. It described a flashing arc in the air. It disappeared to the hilt in the white wolf's side. A fearful howl wailed out upon Agathya's ears.

AGATHYA KNEW—WHAT RUSSIAN PEASANT WOULD not have known?—What would follow. Nevertheless, she stared with bulging eyes at the spectacle that took place within the room. It seemed hardly a second before Sergei held against his lacerated breast the pallid blood-stained face of the Princess Irma Andreyevna Tchernova. He held her so tightly that she could not even struggle, and all the time he laughed terribly, with exultant triumph.

"Mine! Did I not tell you so, my princess? Mine! You would not keep your promise, so I had to make you. Mine! Mine! No one can take you away from me now!"

And indeed, no one could. For even as he cried out, Agathya's staring eyes saw the supple form of her mistress shiver convulsively, then droop limply.

Sergei held the slender figure from him for a moment, and read the unmistakable sign on that pallid face. He carried the relaxed form to a pile of cushions at the center of the room and laid it tenderly down upon the rich velvets and silks, disposing it as gently as if life still dwelt in those white limbs. Then he took out a white handkerchief and made as if to wipe the red stains from that white face.

His hand jerked back; he shook his head. He would leave his blood upon the countenance of the woman he loved. Who can say what his secret thought was, the significance that action held for him? He left her there, and went out of the room.

Still Agathya could not move. She felt that there was more to follow, much more, and that she had to know what it was. She pressed her wrinkled old face against the windowpane, and held tightly to the leash of the animal which she had in charge. The poor beast cowered against her as if in mortal dread.

The door opened, and Sergei entered, both hands full. He was carrying cans from the garage, which was built in under that side of the house. He walked about the room, pouring gasoline generously over the rich rugs, the heaped-up cushions. When he had emptied the cans, he went back to the center of the room and leaned over the jewel-bedecked form lying there.

He sobbed. He cried. He knelt beside the dead woman and kissed her limp hands passionately. He begged for her forgiveness. He railed against her unfaithfulness. Agathya drew back with a shuddering intake of her breath; her own tears welled up and blinded her eyes.

At last Sergei took a matchbox from his pocket and began to strike matches. When they were well ablaze, he flung them on all sides about him.

Hardly had Agathya time to withdraw from the window before the entire room was a blazing inferno. As she staggered away, dragging the gray wolf, the night became lighted by the towering flames that licked their rapid way through the Tehemova residence. The tugging beast at her side pulled in terrified shudders on the embroidered girdle of the doomed Sergei.

One final picture had burned itself into Agathya's very soul. And that was Sergei, standing in the midst of those leaping, roaring flames, his lacerated breast bared, his great arms holding against his bleeding heart the white body of the woman he had loved.

Then Agathya remembered that almost directly under the dining room the garage, with its plentiful stores of gasoline, was situated. When she remembered this, she started to run, pulling the gray wolf with her. Hardly had she reached a safe distance when there came a long rumbling that ended in a roar; the flames had reached the store of gasoline in the garage. When the explosion came, Agathya was thrown to the ground by the shock, and recovered her footing with difficulty, for she was badly shaken.

But throughout it all she held grimly to the girdle at the other end of which pulled the terrified beast which she must not desert, which she must deliver into the right hands at whatever cost to herself. But she turned at the sound of that rumble, that fierce crash, to see the chaos of brilliant and ruthless flame sweeping upward to the very stars at the impetus of that stored gasoline. The Tehemova house had gone, wiped off the face of the earth, and with it had gone Sergei, and the Princess Irma Tehemova, who had lain in her lover's arms only when death had claimed them both.

Close upon the heels of the explosion, Agathya came ringing the bell of the bronze gate, to deliver into the hands of Portia Differdale that most precious and terrible of gifts which she held captive on the girdle of the dead, but triumphant, Sergei.

IV

When I wakened out of my stupid fainting spell and opened my eyes to see the face of Agathya, the truth swept over me again and for a few minutes I could not get the strength to lift my head from the cushions. The old woman had received her orders, apparently, for when she saw my eyes open she rang for Fu, who peered in at the open doorway, smiling cheerily at sight of my questioning gaze.

"Fu call Missee," exclaimed he, disappearing as quickly as he had come.

By the time I had recovered sufficiently to sit up, Portia came in at the doorway and knelt beside me.

"Auntie dear! Forgive me if I didn't stay with you myself, but I knew it was only a fainting spell, and I—"

"You had something more important to attend to," I ventured, dryly, at which my niece's face went rose-color.

I grasped her wrists and whispered somewhat fiercely, I fear, for I had grown very fond of Owen during the weeks of my stay in Meadowlawn:

"Owen? Will he always be—that way?"

She did not need my words to acquaint her with my anxiety.

"Don't worry, dear. Everything will soon be all right, Auntie. He—it—is down in the laboratory, where I am preparing for what must be done."

"But, Portia—?"

"There must be an exorcism, and counteracting spells, and I must wait until about two o'clock this morning before I can begin them, on account of certain conjunctions of the planets, which will be more favorable at that moment."

"You are sure you can do everything without danger to yourself?"

Her face clouded.

" I do not know. But I am willing to give my own life to save Owen," she whispered. Then, "Auntie, if anything happens to me, you must see to it that Owen"—her voice dropped—"that Owen does—not—live—after me."

"Portia!"

"This is imperative. Can't you see why? If I am taken away, and he lives on, with this terrible thing upon him—"

I understood then.

"But if you are successful—?"

"If I am, he will never have this thing come upon him again. You must remember, it was not called upon him by his own evil desires; it was against his conscious will. That changes everything."

I did not pursue the matter farther. Portia probably would not, could not, have told me what my curiosity was inflamed to learn. She remained with me for a few minutes, then went back to the laboratory to prepare for her work.

I got out some of the books we had been consulting those last few days, and read them eagerly, gathering bits of information here and there. What I garnered led me to believe that an attitude of prayer would be the best thing to help my dear niece and poor Owen, so while Agathya watched beside me in the library, I closed my eyes occasionally and let my soul rise in supplication to the Highest Power of all.

Fu padded into the room, and with a deep obeisance, departed. I surprised his comprehending expression, however, and when I later learned that he had spent much of the night before his statue of Confucius, I was grateful. I believe firmly that faithful prayer, whether directed to God in the name of Confucius, or God in the name of the Carpenter, reaches the ear of the Infinite, and releases the God-power that works out so-called miracles.

I expected some bind of supernormal demonstration and was not far wrong. When two o'clock struck, I felt impelled to pray constantly for Portia's success and her escape from the perils that I knew she was surrounded by. Agathya, watching me, suddenly flung herself down upon her old knees and burst out into impassioned, guttural sounds; I knew that she was praying, too, in her poor dumb fashion.

JUST WHAT WENT ON IN the laboratory, I have never asked Portia, for I did not care, afterward, to bring up memories of that terrible time. I know now that she must have had a frightful struggle with the evil influences that had been called by her to undo their evil work in metamorphosing poor Owen. The minutes did drag, that night.

I felt that something awful was hanging over us, as I listened to Agathya's strange, uncouth noises break in upon an otherwise undisturbed silence that weighed upon my very soul. At half past two I opened my eyes with a start, sure that someone, or something, had entered the room with a rush of cold air, but my hasty glance reassured me; we were apparently alone. Yet I did not feel that we were alone. A cold shiver of repulsion went over me. I knew all at once that something inimical was with us, knew it with other senses than those of the body. I sat up straight among the cushions, put the palms of my hands together, and prayed aloud with such fervor as I had never before known.

Portia told me afterward, that at what she judged must have been this hour, she was granted a moment's respite—which she sorely needed—in her battle with that Evil that fought against her for Owen Edwardes' soul. And she knew, somehow, that it was my prayer that had lifted the terrible cloud of Evil from about her, to give her that moment's resting space.

Meantime, as I prayed, something out of the thin air struck at my two hands and forced them down and apart! I cried out. Agathya stopped her strange sounds for a single moment to stare appalled at me, then she began gibbering once more in that awful fashion, seemingly in the last throes of mortal fear. The sight of her groveling on the floor and crying out so horribly, stiffened my Yankee backbone. I forced my two hands together again and held them tightly to my breast, inwardly defying any power inimical to make me cease from my supplications. Nor was I disturbed again. The curtains at the doorway swung and swayed, as if something had passed through with a rush, and the atmosphere of the room became friendly, as it were, once more.

I became aware that a storm was raging. The wind howled and shrieked about the house, beating upon the solid granite as if to tear the blocks apart. In the intervals of the constantly rising gale Agathya's horrible mouthings rose on the night, making it yet more terrible.

Despite it all, I felt strongly impeled to put all thoughts out of my mind save those of prayer, and it is strange that not for a single minute did I doubt Portia's ability to cope with whatever evil stalked abroad that awful night. Not for an instant did I even contemplate going to her assistance; I felt assurance within my heart that I could do more for her by my simple supplication than by my physical presence, ignorant as I was of the occult forces that had been loosed that night.

IT MUST HAVE BEEN ABOUT three o'clock when I heard the storm die down magically, as if calmed by the command of some Mighty One. Shortly afterward I heard the sound of an opening door below, and then voices. Voices—one of them masculine! I dared not stop my prayers, nor did Agathya cease her gabbling noises. When Portia came to the door of the library, she found us both earnestly engaged in supplication, each in her own fashion.

At that happy voice I stopped and dared look toward the door. Portia stood there, leaning on Owen's arm, her face shining with a kind of inward light. Owen withdrew his arm and came toward me, very white but very uplifted.

"God bless you for what you've done tonight, Aunt Sophie," he said to me, reaching out to lift me to my feet. He held me against his heart as if I had been his mother, and kissed me warmly several times.

I could hardly gather my scattered wits. Then, too, I was exhausted by the strain I had been through. I broke down and cried like a child, my head on Owen's shoulder and Portia's arms about us both.

Fu, always ready for an emergency, had prepared a cold supper. He called us from the door, his yellow face ashine as if he, too, had experienced something out of the ordinary. We all went into the dining room and ate like starved things. Agathya refused to sit at the table with us and went into the kitchen with Fu; we could hear him talking to her in a cheerful monologue, and her occasional guttural attempt at speech.

I asked no questions. It did not seem a time for questions. It was a time for rejoicing, and I saw from Portia's air that she was no longer carrying a heavy spiritual burden. Owen was very quiet and subdued, much unlike Ins usual light-hearted self, but the looks he gave Portia every now and then turned my old heart to water with their tenderness.

I insisted that he remain with us the rest of the night, so later we sat and talked—not of the past but of the future.

They had decided to marry the next day, in spite of what people might say to a hasty wedding following close upon the death of Mr. Differdale. The harrowing experience the two had recently undergone had given them clearer vision; they cared nothing for the opinions of outsiders. Their own souls were light and free with the knowledge that they were doing right in taking the step.

So they were married the next morning, Portia and Owen.

V

That they were superlatively happy it is superfluous to say. They insisted that I continue to make my home with them. Portia told me that if it had not been for my prayers she would have succumbed, that last awful night, to the evil powers arrayed against her overwhelmingly, augmented as they were by the subtle mind of the liberated Princess Tchernova. Just when she felt herself failing, of a sudden she had heard my voice praying, and confidence grew strong within her that she would conquer. Fresh courage and strength imbued her efforts, and she held out to the end, the end when Owen resumed his natural form and became once more master of himself. Both she and Owen made me feel that they owed so much to me that they could never repay me, and wished to have me always near them.

We were a happy household. One thing only disturbed me, and this was that Owen became much interested in Mr. Differdale's notes on his work, and began delving into the books so absorbedly that after a few months I was not surprised that he and Portia should take up together the work which my niece had thought to lay aside. The importance of it could not be denied, yet the dangers for them both—. Well, after all, everybody has to live his own life and die his own death.

It was their knowledge of the underlying spiritual causes for the world conflict that led both my dear ones to give their services to their country when we entered the war. Before they went abroad—Owen as an officer and Portia as a nurse—they made over to me all their property, knowing that in case of their deaths I would use it well, as Portia expressed it.

Fu Sing and Agathya served me well during those years, two years that were a harrowing ordeal to me, for my heart was bound up in my dear children. When the news of their deaths came, it found me nursing the old Russian woman on what proved to be her deathbed. Oh, it was as well that I had my hands full of work those days; or how could I have borne it all?

Shortly after Agathya's death Fu was called to China. His filial affection had been appealed to; his old father lying sick desired to see his son before he died. In this way I was desolate and alone; my dear ones taken from me, and those other two who made links with the past, as well.

Mrs. Differdale and Aurora Arnold tried to drop in on me frequently, but I had to discourage their visits; they were so full of neighborhood gossip and the pettinesses of life, that they always left me feeling out of kilter with the world. After a time I found myself entirely alone with my memories, memories both painful and beautiful. It was about this time, while I was so alone, that I began to feel strongly impelled to writing out the experience of that terrible winter.

I did not even try to engage a servant, because I could take care of the house very well myself and the work helped me to keep occupied: it is wise for one who has no real object in life to be busy always. I read a great deal, much that I could not really understand, in Mr. Differdale's books. The reading filled in hours that would otherwise have been unpleasantly empty. And somehow, the more I read and studied, the more I felt impelled to write the story of my experience.

And so at last I started to write down what I remembered of it as best I could, believing that there were those in America who ought to know of that invasion from the dark, with its threat that what has happened once may occur again. It has taken me several months to write these few thousand words, because I have been somehow hindered and have had obstacles thrown in my way, time and time again. I do not believe these hindrances are coincidences; I believe something quite the contrary.

THE THINGS THAT HAVE HAPPENED to prevent me from writing have all been explicable from the standpoint of everyday life, I admit. The fact remains that I have had to fight against interruptions ever since I started to write this account. I had what the doctor called ptomaine poisoning, and had to lie weeks in bed with a trained nurse in attendance. so that afterward I was obliged to fight for sufficient strength to be permitted to use my pen. I have found my telephone connections so strangely broken or unsatisfactory that day after day I was obliged to go out in person to order provisions. Frequently the grocer could not get my order to me and I had to go out for it myself. Always there was a new complication, explicable on perfectly sound material grounds, but resulting in the same thing invariably, i.e., my physical inability to write or impossibility to find time to write.

But now—at last—I have completed my work. I have written to several prominent publishers of fiction magazines, asking them to send me the names and addresses of those of their contributors who, in their opinion, know most about occult matters. I have selected one of these writers and have written her. She is to call here and receive this manuscript, and see to it that it is published and its warning message spread broadcast.

Today is the day she is to come. I shall wrap my manuscript carefully in oiled paper and lock it into a stout metal box. Neither fire nor water must find their way to it. That there will be attempts made to destroy it, I know, but while I live I shall guard it with my life, and I know that the woman whom I have called to take it in charge realizes to the full the gravity of the message and will carry out my wishes in regard to it.

Sophie Delohme
Differdale House,
June 18th, 1924

A Note About the Author

Greye La Spina (1880–1969) was an American author of fantasy and horror fiction. She was a regular contributor to leading pulp magazines of the early twentieth century and over the course of her career wrote over one hundred pieces of fiction with her most notable works being "The Wolf of the Steppes," (1919) and the horror novel, *Invaders From the Dark* (1925).

A Note from the Publisher

Spanning many genres, from non-fiction essays to literature classics to children's books and lyric poetry, Mint Edition books showcase the master works of our time in a modern new package. The text is freshly typeset, is clean and easy to read, and features a new note about the author in each volume. Many books also include exclusive new introductory material. Every book boasts a striking new cover, which makes it as appropriate for collecting as it is for gift giving. Mint Edition books are only printed when a reader orders them, so natural resources are not wasted. We're proud that our books are never manufactured in excess and exist only in the exact quantity they need to be read and enjoyed.

Discover more of your favorite classics with Bookfinity™.

- Track your reading with custom book lists.
- Get great book recommendations for your personalized Reader Type.
- Add reviews for your favorite books.
- AND MUCH MORE!

Visit **bookfinity.com** and take the fun Reader Type quiz to get started.

Enjoy our classic and modern companion pairings!

Classic & Modern

Bookfinity is a registered trademark of Ingram Book Group LLC. © 2023 Bookfinity. All rights reserved.

Printed in the USA
CPSIA information can be obtained
at www.ICGtesting.com
JSHW021525110324
58997JS00004B/238